# REG E. RAT'S BIRTHDAY FUN CENTER AND SAME DAY OUTPATIENT CARE FACILITY

FRANK J. EDLER

*For Corrie, Isa, and G: The only three people I would endure Reg E. Rat's Birthday Fun Center for every time.*

# 1

## AN INVITATION

MORTIMER SUCKED in air and fought off a searing pain in his side. He wanted to double over and cry like a baby. He couldn't risk the embarrassment around all the moms. They were all waiting at the corner for the school bus to arrive. Hell of a time for his kidney stones to grind him up.

This was the worst pain Mortimer had experienced in his life. He'd heard over and over again about how the pains of labor and childbirth are the worst and he would've believed that, until the stabbing pains in his side started an hour ago.

There was an underlying, uncomfortable pain that was persistent. That pain was punctuated by severe bouts of intolerable agony. It felt as though someone strapped a girdle around his waist, cinched it up and then stabbed him over and over again in the same spot. He wished he could collapse and cry as he asked one of the moms waiting at the bus stop if they could be his mommy and make the pain go away.

Mercifully, the bus arrived a minute ahead of schedule today. The children poured off the bus, energized for freedom from their institutionalized learning facility for the day. A few of them leapt off the bus holding test papers with good grades, eager to flaunt to their mother in front of the other mothers. Another kid proudly displayed an odd-looking art project that was some sort of sculpture made out of a wire hanger, string and bird feathers, dyed a color which could never be found in nature.

Mortimer saw that his boy, too, had something in his hand he was just dying to show his father. Mortimer pushed the grueling discomfort aside at the sight of his son, Ichabod, bouncing off the bus.

"Daddy! Daddy!" Ichabod called as he jumped off the bus skipping the last two steps. The bus driver yelled after him not to run. Ichabod ignored the driver, laser focused on showing his dad what all the excitement was about.

"Look, I'm invited to Christopher's birthday party!" he announced, handing over a birthday party invitation printed on glossy card stock.

Mortimer took the invitation to see what all the fuss was about but before he could read any of the details, Ichabod spurted them out.

"It's at Reg E. Rats! Can we go? Can we go?"

Mortimer's heart sank. The pain returned. Reg E. Rat's was the last place on Earth he wanted to spend a Saturday or any day of his life for that matter. If Hell had a basement, Reg E. Rat's Birthday Fun Center was one floor below it.

"It's next Saturday. We're not doing anything. I already asked mom and she said to ask if you could take me."

Damnit! Ichabod knew how to play the game. He reached out to his mom to make sure the coast was clear. His mother cleared the schedule and placed the burden of going to a children's birthday party square on Mortimer. No doubt his wife already took the opportunity to arrange for a spa day with her little group of friends so she could claim she had an appointment and would not be able to go.

He bit his tongue. He wanted to curse his wife, but he'd have done the same thing if Ichabod approached him first. These were the shadow operations nobody ever trained you for when you became a parent.

"Yeah buddy, we can go."

Young little Ichabod jumped and cheered like he'd just won an Olympic gold medal.

Mortimer faked an enthusiastic smile and was thankful he had a week and a half to mentally prepare for this party at Hell on Earth.

# 2

## 'TIL DEATH DO US PART

MORTIMER AND HIS WIFE, Camille, sat up in bed, covers pulled up to their waist, watching a *really good* show streaming on Prime.

Mortimer's mind wasn't on the show. "I can't believe you set me up to take Icky to Reg E. Rat's. You know I hate that place."

Camille sighed and paused the stream. "I thought you were watching this."

"I am."

"No, you're not. You've been sitting there fussing for the past twenty minutes. It's distracting."

"Okay, you're right. This whole birthday party thing has got me worked up. I can't believe you pawned the whole thing off on me."

"Look, I have a doctor's appointment. I've rescheduled it twice now; I can't put it off again."

"You did not! Icky texted you from school and you made sure you rescheduled the appointment before he got off the bus." Mortimer sucked in air and grabbed his side.

"Sounds like someone else needs to make an appointment to see a doctor." Camille said.

Mortimer grimaced and said, "It's just indigestion," through clenched teeth.

"It's just a birthday party, faker. You go in, drop off the present, play a few arcade games, eat some pizza, sing happy birthday and you're out of there. Two hours tops. You'll have the entire rest of the day to yourself.

"No!" Mortimer argued as the pain subsided. "The invitation says it's three hours long. One to four. The whole afternoon will be shot. A half hour to get there and a half hour back plus all the begging to stay. All the indecisiveness over how to spend the five stupid tickets on garbage prizes. I'll be there all day."

Camille rolled her eyes and pointed the remote at the TV to indicate this argument was over.

Mortimer stared blankly at the screen. He loved watching *The Meat Brothers* with Camille. Tonight, he couldn't focus on the show. It was all images played against the background noise of his mind wrestling with the trials and tribulations of a stupid child's birthday party.

*The Meat Brothers* was a great show too. A series about two guys who weren't brothers in real life but had the same long, scruffy looking lumberjack beards who slaughtered animals for a living. Not only did they operate under the premise that they were brothers but also hunters who hunted down their kill before hacking and slashing it up into delicious cuts of meat. None of it was true. They were actors hired to play out this assisted reality series. Like every other reality show, it was complete bullshit.

That didn't matter to Mortimer or Camille. It didn't matter to the 4.5 million households who had streamed *The Meat Brothers* through their various smart devices. *The Meat Brothers* was a cultural phenomenon despite its brutal nature. America just seemed ready to watch Americans hunt, kill and eat uncommon protein.

Mortimer watched the hunt for this week's prey, a wild yak.

He realized he missed them taking down the yak as he refocused on the show. They'd already begun to field dress the animal. It was one of the highlights of each episode.

*How can I convince her to come with me?* Mortimer thought to himself as we watched the innards of the yak steam out in to the frigid Mongolian air when one of the Meat Brothers, Mook, cut open its belly. Wet yak guts spilled onto the rocky grass plain with a plop. *I need moral support for this party. She doesn't get it. This isn't just any kid's birthday party. It's Reg E. Rat's for Pete's sake.*

The other Meat Brother, Kook, laughed like a hyena as he got down on all fours and licked the steaming pile of guts. A section of its intestine jiggled like a dead snake under the influence of his tongue. *I should tell her. If I tell her she'll understand and come along with me. She won't think I'm a weak little child.*

Mortimer was lost back in his thoughts again, missing the part where Mook and Kook grabbed hold of the dehiscent walls of the yak's split belly and tore the carcass open wider with their bare hands. *I was a kid for chrissake! Of course I've been traumatized for life. I'm a grown man and I've got this thing that's embarrassing to admit. I don't want to look weak and frightened in front of my kid. I don't want my wife to expose me for the coward I am.*

Kook dove into gore inside the yak and made like he was bathing in a tub. Mook doubled over with laughter. *I can do this. I can overcome this. It's just a birthday party. Nobody has to know the shit I went through. I can't talk about it, ever.*

Mook grabbed the dead yak by the tail and dragged the carcass, with Kook riding inside, down the hillside as the camera watched them disappear in the distance.

*I will be brave!*

Mortimer yelped like a little school girl when another abdominal pain slashed through his side like the Meat Brothers carving up a yak.

## 3

### ICKY STICKY STICKY ICKY ICKY

ICHABOD SHIFTED IN HIS DESK. Mrs. Hill, his teacher, had stepped out into the hallway to talk to Coach Coz before class started. Ichabod used the extra moments to tell Christopher, who sat behind and one row over from him, that his dad said he could come to the birthday party.

Christopher gave him a thumbs up. Theo, who sat next to Ichabod and one desk in front of Christopher gave Icky a thumbs up. Theo was going to the party as well. Most of the class was going to the party. Everyone in class got an invitation. Everyone except for Mark R.

Mark R. was the class bully. Every class has one. Mark R. hadn't been at the bully game long enough to earn a wicked nickname like Thug or Wart or Snarl. He was just Mark R. because since kindergarten, there were two Marks in their class, Mark R. and Mark E. That was how every teacher every year since kindergarten made it clear which Mark was being called upon.

Ichabod neglected to remember Mark R. sat behind him. He was too excited to let Christopher know he was coming to his birthday party. Mark R. didn't know he wasn't invited until that moment.

Mark R. didn't give anyone a thumbs up. Mark R. scrunched his face up like a fat grizzly bear and asked "What party?" loud enough for the whole class to hear.

Silence filled the room. Ichabod prayed the sudden stop of idle chit chat coming from Mrs. Hill's classroom would raise her suspicions and she would run in to see what the problem was. No such luck. It seemed that when Mrs. Hill was talking to Coach Coz, she was lost in another world, like she liked him or something. Ichabod thought that was odd since Mrs. Hill was married to Mr. Hill.

"It's just a small birthday party," Christopher explained to Mark R.

"Small birthday party? There ain't no such thing as a small birthday party at Reg E. Rat's. That's a big place full of video games and prizes and long birthday party tables and a robot band. I seen it on TV all the time. How come you didn't invite me Chris-toe-durrr?"

Christopher hesitated, searching for a lie. Icky and Theo glanced at each other, frightened for their friend and glad they weren't the targets. Yet.

"M-m-my parents, they said I could only invite a couple of kids from class because my, umm, family is big and they will be there too."

"You can invite me. I'm just one more. What? Is your family poor?"

"N-n-no, just I was only allowed to invite so many of my friends is all."

"Oh, Icky Sticky here," Mark R. reached forward and poked a finger hard into Ichabod's back, "is your friend and I'm not?"

"Ow," Ichabod said because getting jabbed with Mark R.'s thick sausage finger fucking hurt.

"Oh that shit didn't hurt. Quit being such a wuss Icky Sticky."

Christopher saw his opening. Mark R. had his attention on Ichabod now and giggled at Ichabod being called Icky Sticky. Mark

R. loved it when people laughed at what he thought were clever nicknames he tagged on his classmates. He decided to continue harassing Icky Sticky since he got a positive reaction.

"Icky Sticky Sticky Icky Icky." Mark R. said like he'd just written a brilliant poem on the human condition.

"Shut up," was all Ichabod could come up with at the spur of the moment for a comeback.

What he really wanted to say was, *"Shut the fuck up, Mark R. you waste of space. You belong in the trash with all the other garbage. Nobody likes you and everyone wishes you were dead."* But Ichabod knew if he ever said anything even close to something like that, he'd feel worse pain than a poke in the back. It would be a fight after school for sure. Plus, his dad would kill him if he found out Ichabod had used the 'f' word.

"I'll shut up if you let me take your place at Chris-toe-*durr's* birthday party. Also, I won't kick your ass for trying to tell me to shut up Icky Fuckin' Sticky."

"Who just used that word?" Mrs. Hill stood in the doorway to class, wide-eyed with terror that such a terrible word had been uttered in her classroom.

The whole class sat up straight, tight-lipped and eager for Mrs. Hill to get on with the learning so none of them had to rat-out Mark R. as the culprit.

Mrs. Hill cast a suspicious glare on the whole class, row by row, chair by chair as she sauntered back into the classroom. She was looking for the guilty face among them. All she saw was terrified eyes and the condescending grin on this year's class bully, Mark R.

He was always guilty of everything. But the boys around him also carried faces too nervous to be guilty. She decided to hold her glare a moment longer. It would be all the punishment they would need. She would never hear that word in her class for the rest of the school year.

Mrs. Hill turned her back to the class and began bringing up the day's first lesson on the smartboard.

The class let go a sigh of relief.

Mark R. whispered under the din of Mrs. Hill's crow-like lecturing, "Oh, you may as well give me the present you were going to bring to the party since you won't be going now," and he jabbed his meaty finger into Ichabod's back with each of the next two words he spoke, "Icky. Sticky."

# 4

## WAR BOY AND THE LAZER TAZER

MORTIMER TOOK Ichabod to the Toyland Super Center to pick out a present for Christopher's birthday party. He had a target price in his head. No more than fifteen dollars.

The art of shopping for a birthday present had become more complicated in adulthood. When you're a kid you just want to get your friend the coolest present possible without it being so cool that you'd rather have it yourself. But, as the adult who controlled the money, the game was guessing how much the birthday party was costing the host parents on a per child basis. You didn't want to spend more than you were getting out of attending the party.

Mortimer checked out Reg E. Rat's web site before they left and saw the going rate for a standard Reg E. Rat birthday party package was $10.99 per guest. With add-ons and upgrades the figure could climb up to twenty-five bucks per kid.

Mortimer gauged how much Christopher's parents would be willing to spend on the party. He didn't know the parents well enough to understand their financial situation or social inclinations. He'd seen them at parent-teacher conferences and PTO events and that was about it. From that little bit of knowledge he gave leeway for an upgrade to extra game tokens at most. That's how he arrived fifteen dollars and not a penny more.

Father and son entered the toy store, which by name, sounded like it should be an enormous place but the reality was, it was a small mom and pop store tucked in a strip mall. The days of single-minded big box stores were over. The owners gambled on making their business sound more grandiose than the reality of the shop. The locals must have enjoyed that charm because they'd been the go-to toy store in town for many years.

"Okay Ick," Mortimer said as they entered to the jingling of bells clanging against the glass door, "what should we get Christopher? Remember, no more than fifteen dollars."

"I dunno, dad. I guess just a frisbee or a Hot Wheels or something."

Mortimer frowned. Ichabod always liked shopping for birthday presents for his friends. He'd go right for the big ticket items and negotiate his way down to something right at the spending ceiling. Now he was suggesting cheap, thoughtless gifts?

"Frisbee? I thought you and Christopher were good friends?"

Ichabod looked down at his sneakers, "We are. It's just," he paused not knowing how to explain why he didn't want to get Christopher anything cool, "Christopher likes frisbees is all."

"Frisbees huh?" Mortimer wasn't buying it. As much as he'd love to only spend money on a frisbee, he knew something was amiss.

"Oh, look. This bubble blower is neat," Ichabod said, trying to throw his dad off the scent.

"Icky, what's wrong?"

"Nothing. Let's just get this bubble blower. Christopher'll like this."

Mortimer took a knee to talk to his boy face to face. "What's going on, Icky? Tell me."

Ichabod sighed. Dad had figured him out. "There's this kid, Mark R. He wasn't invited to the party and he's mad. And since I was the one who told him about the party, I have to give him my present for Christopher and he's going to go to the party in my place."

Mortimer nodded understanding. "So you want to buy a crappy present since it's going to be from this Mark R. kid."

Ichabod nodded, looking down at his toes again.

Mortimer crooked a finger under his son's chin and raised it to meet him eye to eye. "You are not giving Christopher's birthday present to Mark R. and Mark R. isn't going to Christopher's birthday party. Sounds to me like Mark R. is a bully and I won't let that happen to you. Do you understand me?"

Ichabod nodded. He felt better that his dad had his back but he didn't understand how his dad could keep Mark R. from getting to him at school.

"So, I want you to pick out the best present possible for Christopher, under fifteen dollars, and I assure you, you will be the only one giving that present to Christopher. Deal?"

"Deal," Ichabod said.

"Okay so, what does Christopher *really* want?"

"I dunno. He likes playing War Boy and Fortress Battle Z."

An abdominal pain twisted in his side. His innards didn't like the sound of that price tag. "Well, video games are too expensive. Let's take a look around."

Icky and his dad browsed the aisles and shelves. They checked out action figures which weren't expensive enough and action figure play-sets that were too expensive. There were board games that excited Mortimer but came across as boring to Ichabod. There were some neat STEM kits to make slime or volcanos but they seemed kind of nerdy. Then they got to the guns.

Ichabod lit up when he spied the array of toy guns available. There were guns that shot foam darts and pistols that set-off pop caps. There were blasters from sci-fi movies and rifles from westerns. All of them had bright orange covers over the muzzles and killed the spirit of the toy by making them look obviously fake. All of them, but one.

"Oh yeah! It's a Lazer Tazer just like in the War Boy game! He'll love this!" Ichabod said, pulling the gun off the peg to try it out.

The gun was mounted to a cardboard display backing but you could manipulate the trigger and other bells and whistles on the toy. Ick pulled the trigger and the gun crackled and vibrated. There was a slide mechanism that made an ominous sound of the gun being cocked and loaded. There was a scope that must look cool when peered through, because Ichabod said, "Oh cool!" when he squinted into it.

War Boy was a video game about a kid who found himself in the middle of a mutant war. He used his trusty Lazer Tazer, a gun that shot supercharged laser-lighting, to kill off the mutant army and save the world. Boys loved it. Parents somehow rationalized the gun was okay since it shot fake lasers instead of fake bullets.

Mortimer checked out the price on the peg while Ichabod fiddled with it. $14.99, perfect!

They'd found the present.

Mortimer was happy to see his son out of the doldrums. When they made their purchase at the counter, Mortimer grabbed a birthday card off a display next to the register.

"Why'd you get a card, Dad? We're not giving Christopher a gift card." Icky asked.

"Ich, my mother taught me to always give a card with a present. It doesn't matter if it's a birthday or a holiday. If you give someone a present, it should always come with a card. And, you should always write something personal in the card."

"Like how I hope Christopher has a kick ass birthday party and thinks my present is the best?"

Mortimer laughed and mussed up Ich's hair, "Yeah, something like that but without the ass part."

## 5

### THE CALM BEFORE THE STORM

MORTIMER AND CAMILLE lay in bed watching the new episode of The Meat Brothers. They were plugging away at nutria. Mortimer and Camille had never heard of nutria, horse-sized rats that plagued spillways and canals of coastal Louisiana towns.

The Meat Brothers were patrolling a canal in some unnamed town. Mook drove a beat up, brown pick-up truck of some nondescript make and model along a drainage canal. Kook knelt in the bed of the truck, his trusty two-shot at the ready. A giant brown rodent on the opposite bank of the canal made a dash down to the water when it became uncomfortable with the presence of the pick-up. Kook blasted the varmint and it tumbled, dead, into the water.

The camera zoomed in on the carcass as it bobbed, lifeless, in the murky water.

"I don't wanna go," Mortimer said.

"Shh, this is the good part," Camille said.

"Woo! You plugged him good!" Mook hollered as he hit the brakes and hopped out of the cab of the pick-up.

"I can't. I can't do this Reg E. Rat thing. Any other birthday party

I'll go to for the rest of our lives, just not this one. Please, Camille," Mortimer pleaded as a bead of sweat formed on his brow.

"We have to do this now? Look! He's running in the water to get the nutria. Gosh, look how big that thing is," Camile said, trying to maintain focus on the show.

"Aww, gawd! She's a beaut! I'm pretty sure she's with pup. Some lucky guy knocked her up real swell!" Kook said as he floated on the dead nutria carcass like it was an innertube in a pool. He kicked his feet to float it to the bank where Mook was waiting to land their prize.

"Torture! Torture! I'd do anything to trade places with that rat right now."

"It's a nutria."

"It's lunch!" Mook hailed as he pulled and Kook pushed the giant hairball out of the canal.

Mortimer experienced the worst stabbing pain since it started. He cried and curled up into the fetal position, clutching at his stomach like his innards were about to fall out like a gutted nutria.

"What's wrong?" Camille screamed, kicking off the covers and hovering over Mortimer but hesitant to touch him as he grunted in agony.

"I'm dying!" he managed to say, pain running through like a dull sword through his side.

"Maybe you need to go to the bathroom?" Camille said, hopeless to give any sort of real advice.

The word bathroom made him realize the pain did feel like terrible bowel contractions. Maybe he did have to go to the bathroom. He wasn't sure how he was going to make it there though. The pain was unbearable.

"Yeah. Ahh. Gonna shit right here. Can't move." He grunted, having made an executive decision without giving any real thought to the logistics and terrible aftermath that decision would cause. He wasn't thinking much of anything other than how he was going to get the pain to subside.

If the pain lasted much longer, he was going to pass out without a doubt. He tried to relax his bowel as his wife screamed in protest. But his guts were too wound up, like his intestines had a charlie horse that wound up tighter and tighter.

Camille jumped out of bed. She grabbed her cell phone, intent on calling 9-1-1 but found her fingers were jittering too much to operate the phone.

Mortimer fell silent. The pain had washed away like ocean water washing back out to sea after crashing to shore.

He gulped for air like he'd just run a marathon.

"It passed," he said between breaths.

"We need to get you to the hospital, now," Camille said, putting down her phone and grabbing her purse.

"No! No, no. No. I'm okay. I promise."

"I've never seen you in so much pain, Mort."

"I just... need... to fart," Mortimer said, getting his breath back.

"Fart? You expect me to believe that was all over a fart? There's something wrong, Mort. You need to get it checked out."

"Okay," Mortimer pleaded. "Okay, but not tonight. If I go tonight then who will take Ick to the party tomorrow?"

"Oh, now all of a sudden you want to go to the party?"

"I can't let Ick down. We..." he paused not wanting to talk about the bully, "we have a plan."

"A plan? A plan for what?"

"A plan for having a good time."

"I don't understand why you have to have a plan for a good time. It's not for you; It's for Ick and his friends."

"It's not that. It's the place. I'm terrified of that place."

"You're being ridiculous. It's just a kid's birthday party. Nothing else."

"Just a kid's birthday party? That place is terrifying! It's all injury inducing video games, cardboard surplus pizza, a maniacal monster robot band and the rat. Camille, the icon of the place is a rat! They serve food there!"

"Morty, you're overreacting. Look at you. That pain has got you in cold sweats."

"I'll go and get the party over with and then I'll make an appointment to see the doctor."

"No, you go to the party with Ick and have a good time. I'll make you an appointment while I'm at the doctor's office tomorrow. " Thank you, sweetie. That's a help."

"You're welcome. Just promise me one thing?"

"What's that?"

"Don't eat the pizza there. I don't think your stomach will be able to handle it."

"Ugh, just thinking about it hurts."

"Let's get some sleep," Camille said. "We've all got a big day tomorrow."

## 6

LIVING THE RAT LIFE

"Alright, Rory, it's your shot at the big time," Wendy called out. "I need you to be The Rat."

Rory Guzman didn't want to be The Rat. He just wanted to put in his eight hours and get out of this place. He never saw himself working at Reg E. Rat's Birthday Fun Center as a young impressionable child. Yet, here he was, bussing ransacked tables after each round of birthday parties had run through the place. And now he was being told he needed to be Reg E. Rat himself.

That wasn't a job for him. That was a job for the still-wet-behind-the-ears, over enthusiastic theater types that came through the door looking for a part time gig. He didn't want to put on the suit and make a fool of himself.

His manager had other ideas.

Rory would've quit there if he wasn't in a no-win situation in his life. This was the summer before he started college. Just one more month to go and he'd be out of the state and away from this town. He couldn't quit now; he needed the money and he would never find a new job in time to make up for the lost income switching jobs. He had to ride out Reg E. Rat's until September, then he could move away and find a better part time gig near the university to work between classes.

"C'mon, Rory. Do it and lunch will be on me today. Please," Wendy, the shift manager, begged.

"But, I dunno the routine or anything."

He knew the routine. He'd watched Reg E. Rat perform his birthday show four times a day, three times a week for the past six months. He knew every line of the pre-recorded Reg E. Rat Birthday Fun Center show that played over the P.A. He knew every hand gesture, every dance step. He knew it because it was designed to be easy to learn and retain.

The entire birthday party spectacle had been created by the corporate masterminds at Reg E. Rat's Birthday Fun Center and Same Day Outpatient Care Facility, Inc. Rory once asked the store manager what the second part was all about. The manager shrugged and told him it was some sort of parent company and not to worry about it.

Rory didn't give it another thought. He didn't care if the company wanted to call itself Terrible Pizza and Low Grade Entertainment Company as long as he got paid every Friday.

Rory trudged off to the wardrobe room. Wardrobe was a dank closet that contained the suit. Thirty years in business and they still used the original suit. Never in its history had it been sent to the dry cleaners. One rat, hundreds of bodies.

There was a training DVD that could be played on a tired old TV/VCR player combo that was nearly as old as the Reg E. Rat costume. Rory decided to skip it. It was just a rat costume. There couldn't be much to it.

Reg E. Rat is a brown rat that sports a red, yellow and blue propeller beanie and a blue sleeveless t-shirt with the initials 'RR' in bold white letters embroidered on the chest. He wears oversized Yellow Crocs for shoes. Rory heard the original shoes were big yellow sneakers that had fallen apart beyond repair. The Crocs were said to have been bought for a dollar at some yard sale.

Rory wasn't sure how true the story was. He always remembered the rat in the commercials wearing the gaudy yellow Crocs. Maybe it was The Mandela Effect?

Rory stepped inside Reg E. Rat's legs, which were just overalls. He had to be delicate about slipping his legs in because he could see the costume was becoming threadbare, already torn and patched in several places. He slipped on the Crocs over his socks. Then he pulled on Reg E.'s hands (which were just gloves that smelled like the inside of an old baseball mitt) and slid the torso over his head. There was a hole in the armpit. He'd make a mental note not to raise his hand too high when he waved. Finally, he donned Reg E. Rats stuffy head piece and he was suddenly every child's favorite birthday party rodent.

He wished the mirror in the wardrobe room wasn't so scratched up and covered with punk rock band stickers. He might've been able to see himself and mimic some gestures to get a feel for the character.

Screw it, as long as he played along, he'd get paid.

He opened the door ready to be Reg E. Rat for the first round of birthday parties.

He walked down the hallway that led back to the party hall. One of the cooks, dressed in an all-white jacket and pants smeared with pizza sauce, gave him a high five and said, "Let's get a good body count today."

Rory thought that was an odd way to say 'break a leg' or 'have a good show' but it must have been some shop speak the kitchen people had. When you cooked food as awful as Reg E. Rat pizzas, there was a tendency to be as off as the food.

He found the door just before the party hall marked, "Backstage Access. Crew Only."

He walked through the door and was ready for the show to begin.

# 7

## WHY'D YOU BRING A SHOTGUN TO THE PARTY?

MORTIMER COULDN'T REMOVE his hands from the steering wheel. He gripped it so tight it threatened to crumble to dust in his palms. He didn't know which hurt worse, the pain in his sides or the pain of attending a Reg E. Rat birthday party.

"Dad, can we go in now?" Ichabod asked.

They arrived at Reg E. Rat's Birthday Fun Center fifteen minutes early for the party. Mortimer had no intention of going in any sooner than the scheduled start time of 1 p.m. He would've gone in at 3:59 p.m., one minute before the end of the party but his son would have claimed a childhood of suffering and mistreatment if he chose that route.

"We've got a few minutes. Hold on." Mortimer said, trying to erase the anxiety from his voice.

"Let's just go in now. I can get the seat next to Christopher if we get in early."

Mortimer rolled his eyes. Another disappointment he couldn't allow his son. He took a deep, deep breath and let it out, slowly. His hands would not let go of the wheel. His mind tethered him to the car like a boat anchored in a squall.

"Dad?"

"Yeah, yep. Ok, let's go in."

Mortimer had to fight himself to let go of the steering wheel. He unlatched his seatbelt and opened the door. "You got the present?"

Ichabod held it up, triumphant. "Yup! Right here! You have the cards?" Ichabod asked with a chuckle.

Mortimer held up the two birthday cards, one in a white envelope, the other in a pink envelope. "Yup! Right here."

The thought of helping his son get back at this Mark R. kid propelled him out of the car in the face of his anxieties over the birthday party place. He took his son's hand and together they crossed the parking lot to the front door of Reg E. Rat's Hell-Hole on Earth.

There was a bit of a line to get inside. That was the first thing that annoyed Mortimer. There shouldn't be a line to get into what amounted to a crappy pizza place. But Reg E. Rat's made this big production out of child safety, branding each child with invisible ink and then branding the parent with the same invisible mark of the devil. Mortimer didn't know if it was the mark of the devil he and Ichabod would be branded with but, since he'd never actually seen the invisible branding under the blacklight, he could only assume that when you were in Hell, they tarnished you with the mark of the devil. Logic would dictate, right?

The branding station caused the line. Each child and subsequent parent had to be tagged together. It was a process. There was a half-wall divider, the left side of the wall being the entrance line to get in and the right side of the wall being the exit queue to leave. There was no line to get out.

"Roaches check in but they don't check out," Mortimer said aloud.

The woman standing in front of them turned and cast him a wicked glare. She didn't seem to appreciate his dark humor. Mortimer shrugged and said to the lady, "Shoot me."

Screw her if she didn't like his comment. Then he spied a sign mounted on the wall and thought he'd made a drastic miscalculation in his dismissive comment to the woman.

*No Firearms* the sign read, with the silhouette of a .357 Magnum in a black circle with a red line slashed through it.

"What the fuck?" Mortimer said aloud.

"Sir! There are children present!" The lady in front of him said, her voice an octave higher than it ought to be.

Everyone in line got quiet and stared at him with daggers.

Mortimer was embarrassed. He wasn't one to use the 'F-word' in public. He barely used it in casual conversation among friends. He couldn't help it, the *No Firearms* sign was so absurd and out of place in a children's birthday party place. Why on Earth would they need a sign like that? Was there a gun problem that crept into the dark part of the American birthday party experience that he wasn't unaware of?

"Dad, you said the F-word out loud." Ichabod whispered to him.

Mortimer felt awful. He was very adamant about his son not using bad words ever. He didn't want to hear his son say anything even slightly off color. He would not let Ichabod call people dumb or stupid. He admonished Ichabod for saying he *hated* anything. "You don't hate anything, you just dislike it. Hate is too strong a word," he would tell Ichabod.

Now he'd crossed a major line. He used one of the crescendo words. One of the big five. One of the words that would cost Ichabod a year of hard grounding. No TV, no video games, no internet. Just books for twelve months.

"We'll discuss it after the party," was all Mortimer could think to offer as an explanation to his boy.

Ichabod got quiet after that. The entire line did. They all waited uncomfortably to get inside before the wild town cusser went off in a deluge of filth again.

When they reached the official Reg E. Rat brander/greeter/hostess, she asked whose party they were attending and stamped the devil's sigil on both Ichabod and Mortimer. "And Sir, kindly refrain from the use of bad language while you're in this establishment. Reg E. Rat is terribly sensitive to that type of speech. Also, we've had several complaints already about your language. Enjoy the party!"

8

## PARTY HEARTY MR. SMARTY

Ichabod found the area of tables reserved for Christopher's party. Christopher was there a few moments ahead of Ichabod and his dad. Ichabod ran up to Christopher and handed him his present with excited eyes. Christopher and his parents pepped up when their first guest arrived.

Christopher's mother took the present and placed it in a giant garbage bag on the floor. She nodded politely to Mortimer and thanked him for coming. She invited Ichabod to take a seat next to Christopher. That made Ichabod's day. Any concerns he had about the birthday party were forgotten. He was all smiles now.

Christopher's father, who Mortimer had not yet met, approached Mortimer and offered a handshake and a welcoming pat on the shoulder.

"Hey, thanks for coming. I'm Christopher's dad, Gabe."

"Hey, Gabe," Mortimer said, grabbing hold of Gabe's hand, "I'm Mortimer, Ichabod's dad."

"Morty! Alright!"

Mortimer didn't like it when people assumed it was okay to call him Morty, like they've been pals forever. He introduced himself as Mortimer. What's so hard about saying Mortimer?

Mortimer ground his teeth into an uncomfortable smile, "Gabey!" he said.

Gabe chucked, unimpressed with the nickname he was given in return. "Right. Right. Well, hang out. Everyone else will be here soon."

Another guest arrived to save them both from the uncomfortable small talk that was about to ensue now that they knew they didn't like one another. Gabe excused himself to greet the newcomer.

Mortimer stood behind his son's chair.

"I get to sit next to Christopher!" Ichabod said as if he won an award.

"That's awesome, Ick," Mortimer said, continuing with the theme of nicknames.

It didn't take long for all the guests to arrive. Soon, the tables for Christopher's party filled with kids ready for the party of the century.

Mortimer felt the urge to pee rise above the undercurrent of constant uncomfortable pain he'd been experiencing all day. He told Ichabod he was going to run to the bathroom and to stick with Christopher until he got back.

Mortimer found a hallway with the word *RESTROOMS* painted over the corridor. He wound through the throngs of children and parents to get to the bathroom. The hall was long with a bunch of doors on both sides. One said, *BACKSTAGE, EMPLOYEES ONLY*. Another said, *KITCHEN STAFF ONLY*. There were a few more that weren't marked but were probably storage closets or small offices. The Boys' and Girls' Restrooms were at the end of the hall.

Mortimer felt weird entering a room marked *BOYS*. It made him feel like a kid toucher or something but it wasn't as if there were any doors marked *MEN*. As he pushed the door open a quick, sharp pain stabbed his side. He wanted to cry. Maybe he was a boy.

Mort hobbled over to the urinal. The pain went from a stab to a throb. He hoped it only meant he had to pee.

There was urgency in his bladder but the piss wouldn't come. He tried to push but that intensified the discomfort in his side. Mort prayed a prayer to the God he infrequently spoke to and asked for sweet relief. God seemed to be busy with other worshipers who were thoughtful enough to speak with him on a more regular basis. His prayer was lost in a long queue.

He felt the tip of his dick burn as if the piss were right there, too afraid to jump. He tried relaxing everything. A drip dropped out and tapped the plastic basket in the urinal that once contained a pleasant smelling deodorizer, which had dissolved long ago. A drop, it was a start.

Mort tried to relax even more. He could feel the sensation of pee all up inside himself but still he could not empty his bladder. He wanted to zip up and admit defeat but he felt like he'd put a lot of effort into this and he didn't want it to go to waste.

Mort stood there for far too long. If he waited for the piss to come much longer, everyone would think he slinked away to drop a deuce. He didn't want his son's friends' parents thinking he was the kind of dad that would poop in a seedy joint like Reg E. Rat's. That would be uncivilized. The only people who defecated in bathrooms like this were derelicts and hobos.

Why didn't Reg E. Rats have a *NO HOBOS* sign in the foyer? Mortimer could only assume management encouraged bums to come take dumps in their bathrooms if that was the case.

The piss started to flow. Slow, but with mercy. It didn't bring relief. To Mort, it felt as if someone half-opened the valve. And there was a strong, pungent smell to the piss as well.

Maybe this was some kind of urinary tract infection. It would make sense. He'd had them before. Some hot pee, difficult to get going and lasted a day or so. Never with this much pain accompanying it but maybe that was part of getting old. At least he had a self-diagnosis now. He could get some antibiotics from the doctor and be right as rain.

Mort zipped up and flushed. He scrunched his nose at the foul smell from his pee. It was kind of awful, like something was dead in his groin. He washed up and returned to the party before anyone could accuse him of evacuating his bowels.

Mortimer noted at least five other birthday parties were taking place. It made the place feel like a birthday party sweatshop. This place ground 'em out like a factory. He couldn't imagine a parent not loving their child to such a degree that they would give them a birthday party as soulless as a Reg E. Rat's party.

Music began to play over the PA system. It was fun music, too fun in fact. It was Muzak on Prozac. A Reg E. Rat employee took the stage in front of all the simultaneous birthday parties. She was dressed in clothes that looked just like Reg E. Rat's except they were human sized. She looked ridiculous. She also looked like she knew she looked ridiculous.

"Hey gang! I'm Jessica, your party hostess with the mostest! Do you know what time it is?" she asked.

Mortimer could tell she was supposed to deliver that opening with a great deal of enthusiasm and mystery to peak everyone's interest. The girl delivered the line like she was in a bad third grade presentation of Xanadu.

"I can't hear you," Jessica said.

She heard everyone, but she had to say the disingenuous line anyway. Corporate policy.

"It's time for the birthday party!" Jessica waited for applause and cheer that never came.

"And who are we here celebrating today?"

About a hundred kids all yelled out six different names at the same time. Well, that must have made each of the birthday kids feel super special.

Jessica the Party Hostess jumped off the stage and approached Christopher. "Hey there Mr. Birthday Boy!" She knew he was the birthday boy because he was marked with an oversized inflatable yellow, blue and red birthday crown, the same as the trademark colors of Reg E. Rat's signature beanie.

"Hi," Christopher said, embarrassed by the attention.

"It's not a birthday party until a certain someone comes to celebrate. Do you know who that certain someone is, Birthday Boy?"

"Reg E. Rat?" Christopher asked, unsure if that was the correct answer.

"That's right! Let's get Reg E. Rat out here to celebrate! Time to party hearty, Mr. Smarty!" Jessica exclaimed more to the room than Christopher himself. Jessica bopped Christopher on his crown, pushing it down over his face.

Everyone had a great laugh over the birthday prank. Everyone except Christopher.

## 9

### RAT-TAT-WA-HOOEY

Rory wrestled with the curtain as his entrance music played.

He couldn't feel the seam with his gigantic furry rat hands on. He swatted and swatted until he saw daylight poke through the part in the curtains through his Reg E. Rat head and shoved himself through before he lost it again.

As soon as Rory was center stage, the kids started screaming. Most screams were in excitement, but he'd heard a few of terror among the youngest of the audience.

He realized he was fixated on the unexpected reaction from the crowd and missed his cue when his pre-recorded voice began playing over the loudspeakers. He was supposed to be gesturing along with Reg E. Rat's big hello speech.

Rory waved his hands around a bit trying to remember the moves and sync them up to the part of the speech he was at now. He didn't expect the speech to be so muffled through the Reg E. Rat head. He knew he must have looked like an idiot the way he saw the kids all staring at him, dumbfounded, through his black mesh eyes.

Rory did the best he could. He couldn't wait for this to be over.

He swiveled his hips and pointed at specific kids in the crowd. He threw both hands in the air. He pumped his fist a time or two and even spread out his arms like he was ready to hug the whole room. The truth was, he had no idea if any of those gestures were being made at the right moment but they were all things he'd watched the other Reg E. Rat players do all the time.

He heard party music begin to play. Reg E. Rat's speech was over. Everyone applauded. Most kids were smiling. Rory guessed, somehow, he'd done a passable job. So far.

When the music started playing Reg E. Rat was supposed to return backstage and then re-enter the party room through a side door in a few minutes. While he was backstage, the party hosts were passing out paper cups full of game tokens to each of the kids.

The kids were sent off to the game room to play games and Reg E. Rat was supposed to mingle among the crowds. A regular meet and greet and pictures with the celebrity rat. This was the most harrowing time for a Reg E. Rat player.

Face time with the kids meant tons of questions, opportunities to yank on the costume to test the authenticity of how real the rat was. There were always a few jerky kids in the crowd that would flat out kick and punch Reg E. Rat so they would be legendary in school for the next six months.

Rory took a deep breath. He wanted to remove the helmet and get a fresher breath of air but policy dictated he stay in the suit until the entirety of his performance was completed. Some corporate bigwig that never donned the suit once in their lives felt that, from where they stood on the top floor of their corner office in a corporate tower of whichever mega city Reg E. Rat Corporate Headquarters was situated, being locked up in the suit helped keep the player in character. This was a franchised birthday party mill not Shakespearean theater.

But Rory just wanted to get through this day and a few more, get paid and leave for college, so he played along inside the smelly head.

Wendy, the shift manager, burst through the door to the backstage area. "You're a minute late. On the game room floor, now!" she spat.

"Are you sure nobody else can do this? I screwed the dance up so bad. I can't do this."

Wendy looked him straight in the Rat eyes, which was weird because she wasn't actually looking at him in his own eyes so the seriousness with which she said the following lost a lot of its umph. "You got this, Rory. You're doing great. Get out there, get a few pictures and don't forget, the only thing you're allowed to say is—"

"—Rat-Tat-Wa-Hooey," Rory said, filling in the blank without the expected enthusiasm.

"Right! Rat-Tat-Wa-Hooey! Like that, with lots of pep and shoot a fist in the air when you say it, too. You got this Rory!"

"I got this, Rory," Reg E. Rat said and marched into his next battle, reluctant and unsure of himself.

# 10

## THE KILLER BEES

It wasn't that Camille didn't want to go to the birthday party. She would've gone with Ick in a heartbeat and saved her husband the torment. She didn't think it was going to be as big a deal as Mortimer made it out to be. She had an appointment to keep though. She couldn't put it off or she would chicken out. Again.

She told Mortimer it was just a standard well visit to the doctor. That was kind of true. She *was* well. She was going to a doctor, of sorts. Just not your standard, run-of-the-mill family practitioner. She was going to the plastic surgeon.

More specifically, she was going to see a plastic surgeon that specialized in the type of surgery she was in the market for. That plastic surgeon she was referred to by the first plastic surgeon she consulted with about her little problem

Camille had an image problem. Always had. It dated all the way back to middle school. Camille always felt like she was last. Last to have been kissed. Last to have a boyfriend. Last to have sex. Last to get engaged. And, last to grow tits, if you could even call them grown.

Yes, it was probably the most fickle of all the lasts but she struggled with it her whole life. Most guys didn't mention her small breasts. They didn't have to. She spent her whole life seeking any attention a guy might have paid her. And when the rare guy did notice her, she'd lose him to the first girl who came around with a bigger rack. Until she met Mort.

Mort had an authentic appreciation for Camille's small breasts. She believed he was a rare mutant who preferred small breasts over big ones. He was never distracted by larger breasts. She noticed when his eyes would wander, they would wander to other small-breasted women. She was endeared by that predilection.

Of course, that wasn't the only reason she married Mortimer. It wasn't even a major reason but it was a part of the whole package.

Still, once the hot and heavy led into legitimate love and their life-long commitment to one another, she found that Mortimer's appreciation to the less than ample breasts she was blessed with wasn't enough. She felt awful for coveting bigger breasts. She wrestled with the desire to get breast implants.

She reached forty and couldn't wait any longer. She needed the boost in self-esteem. It was that or the psychiatrist. She opted for the plastic surgeon instead.

Camille didn't want to make a big deal out of it with Mort. She knew he would only try to talk her out of it. And he would if she gave him a chance to argue the point.

It didn't matter. It would only eat away at her and she would be back to wanting to get the procedure done.

She was only going from an A to a B. That's how she rationalized her decision. Big enough for a boost in self-confidence but not so big that it might turn Mortimer off. She was sure that if she went to a C it would spell certain doom for her marriage. She didn't want that. This was for her and her alone. She needed to do this. She needed some shadows to be cast between her cleavage.

She arrived for her appointment at the Same Day Outpatient Care Facility fifteen minutes early. A coy smile pursed her lips when she passed the Reg E. Rat's on the drive over. She didn't realize how close the surgery center was to where her son and husband were at the birthday party. The building seemed like it was right behind Reg. E Rat's.

Camille checked in with the receptionist. She was nervous. Because the plastic surgeon was a referral, she wasn't familiar with him at all. This would be the first time they would consult. Not much of a consultation, he would mark up her breasts with a Sharpie, knock her out and rip into her with his scalpels. Seemed impersonal but she was past the point of no return now.

After filling out the obnoxious patient check-in forms and returning them to the receptionist, she returned to her seat in the lobby. It seemed crowded for a surgery center. Did they really schedule like a dozen people for breast enhancements at once? She hoped this wasn't some kind of tit mill or something.

Couldn't be. There must be all manner of surgeons that operate here. It wasn't Boobs R Us; it was an Outpatient Care Facility. All types of procedures must be conducted here.

Hell, maybe they even had a butcher, she quipped to herself. She picked up a women's magazine and read up on the fifteen things to do to spice up your marriage.

## 11

BULLY AND THE BEASTS

Ichabod held a paper cup full of Reg E. Rat Birthday Fun tokens. The weight of the tokens in the cup was impressive. He felt like there was an endless supply in his hand. Ichabod was too young to understand that the Reg E. Rat Birthday Fun tokens were a psychological tool used by corporations to lure little kids into harassing their parents into spending more money on video games than they would in a regular arcade.

The tokens were designed to weigh more than a U.S. Quarter. This way, to the kids, it felt as if they had a bottomless supply and could play the hell out of all the games before it would ever end. What they didn't realize until they were whipped up into an arcade game-playing frenzy was that all but the most boring of games cost at least two tokens to play (if not three or four for the really high-end stuff.)

Before they knew it, they blew their entire token supply on some dumb games and had a few dumb prize tickets they could turn in for prizes that brought disappointment and disillusionment.

And the prize tickets were a whole other racket. Only half the games in the Reg E. Rat Birthday Fun Arcade dispensed prize tickets. So, to maximize your token to ticket ratio you had to dedicate your whole paper cup of tokens to playing only the games that dispensed tickets. When it comes to kids, they'd rather play one of those video games with a gun or blaster attached to it than some boring, ancient looking midway game where you roll a ball into a hoop.

Then when you did stumble across one of those games and realized the tickets were involved, you would only get one to three tickets per token. Kids don't have a grasp on token-to-ticket-value ratios the way Reg E. Rat Birthday Fun Center has bean counters to run the algorithms and maximize profits. So, they plug tokens worth less than a quarter into arcade games that spit out tickets that are worth less than a penny in value once they are cashed in for overvalued prizes at the prize counter.

The whole scheme is sadistic. It should be enough to ward off any loving parent and yet the place is packed, like a Japanese bullet train, every weekend. Especially with kids like Mark R.

Ichabod spotted Mark R. walking in past the hostess. He didn't have a parent or guardian with him. That made him appear even more menacing to Ichabod.

Ick panicked, like a bear cub wandering too far from the protection of its parents. He looked around desperate for the safety of his father. He hated himself for being scared but instinct took over when he spotted Mark R.

He almost cried when he saw his dad looking around for him as well. He tried to play it cool but he speed-walked to his dad.

"Dad. Dad, Mark R. is here!" Ichabod said, a bit winded.

"He is? Where?"

Ichabod didn't dare point and out himself as a scaredy cat. Instead he side glanced in Mark R.'s direction and said, "He's over there by the party table."

Mortimer looked over and saw a kid looking over the collection of birthday presents at Christopher's table. That had to be Mark R. When someone tells you there is a bully, the image of a fireplug of a boy comes to mind. Almost always a boy, especially when it's a boy being bullied. The bully usually has unkempt hair and dresses like their parents don't care what they wear in public. And bullies scowl, all the time. They scowl and sneer and drool.

That's how Mortimer spotted Mark R. He looked every bit like the classic bully. He was a size larger than Ick and the rest of the kids in his class. He wasn't a fireplug per se but Mark R. wasn't as scrawny as the rest of the boys. He looked like he should be a grade or two ahead of Ichabod and his friends. And maybe, he was.

Bullies were often the kids who got held back a grade or two. Always acting out as a result of their shortcomings.

Mortimer told Ichabod to stick close to Christopher and play games. He was going to make sure Mark R. wasn't over there stealing any presents.

Mortimer snuck up on Mark R. as he peeled back the corner of a wrapped present. "Whatcha up to, Mark?"

Mark R. was cool as ice. "Trying to figure out which present is mine," he said without even turning to look at Mortimer.

"Well, none of those are yours, sporto. You're not the birthday boy."

Mark R. tore another corner of another present. "I know that, dumbass. I can't remember which one is the one I'm giving to Christopher."

"Let's cut the crud," Mortimer said, placing his hand on Mark R.'s shoulder and spinning him to meet Mortimer eye to eye, "we both know you didn't show up with a present and I'm not going to let you hijack one that isn't your own."

"Mind your own business, pops!" Mark R. told Mortimer, yanking his shoulder away from the old man's grasp.

"Look, buddy, I'm not trying to bust you. I want to help you out."

Mark R. furrowed his eyebrows. "What the hell are you talking about, old man?"

"You and I both know stealing someone else's present isn't cool. You wouldn't like it if someone did it to you."

"Impossible. No one gives me presents. It would never happen. Not worried."

"It's a jerk move."

The name-calling grabbed Mark R.'s attention.

"That's right," Mortimer continued, "you're a jerk. I know that bugs you. I've got a way out," he told Mark R. pulling out a sealed envelope from inside his jacket.

"What's that?"

"It's a present. From you to Christopher. You can stay at this party and your friends won't think you're a jerk."

"Who the hell are you?"

"Just someone trying to help you out," Mortimer said, offering the card over to Mark R. "Here, take it. No strings. It's got a gift card inside. You could run out of here and use it for yourself or you can invest in not being an idiot and give in to Christopher and have all these kids look at you differently from now on."

Mark R. took the card and looked at it. Not just looked at it, but considered it. His big, dumb oaf facade became transparent and Mortimer saw a scared boy who was given a way out of a life he wasn't fond of living.

Mark R. squeezed the card, feeling for the hard plastic of a gift certificate. He smiled at Mortimer when he felt the small plastic rectangle. "Visa?"

"Does it matter?"

"Yeah, it does."

"Guess we'll just have to wait to find out when Christopher opens it," Mortimer said.

Mark R. stared at Mortimer. Both were wondering if the other would break.

Before either could crack, loud music began to blare over the sound system and a pre-recorded voice beckoned the children in the arcade to return to their seats. The jolly female voice indicated that the world's most famous robot band, The Beasts, were about to put on a special birthday concert. Her voice also indicated she was getting paid a handsome stipend for pretending to be that ecstatic about a robot band that performed that same act twenty times a day, seven days a week and had been doing so for decades.

Mortimer walked away from Mark R. as kids flooded the birthday party area once more. He spotted Ick returning with Christopher from the arcade. Ick had a stuffed pizza in his hand that he held out like he'd hit the jackpot in Vegas.

"Dad! Dad! Look what I won!"

"That's awesome, Ick! How'd you win that?"

"The claw machine! I was watching Vanessa try and try and try and she finally ran out of tokens so I put my tokens in and I got it on the first try!"

"That's because I nudged it to a good spot for you," a little girl across the table from them said, none too pleased.

Mortimer assumed her to be Vanessa.

Ichabod didn't say anything. He clutched the stuffed pizza slice close to his chest.

Jessica, the world's least motivated party hostess, turned on the mic and said in her most apathetic tone, "Okay, all you party animals, find your seats because it's almost time for Reg E. Rat's favorite rock and roll band, The Beasts!"

"I can't believe we're going to get to see The Beasts live in person!" Ichabod exclaimed over his shoulder to his dad.

Mortimer felt the pain in his side return with a vengeance. It wasn't because one of his worst fears was about to come true, it was because the smell of pizza began to waft through the air.

His innards were not ready. Someone was about to stoke the flames of Hell and Mortimer felt like he was trapped in the oven.

## 12

PIZZA PARTY PANDEMONIUM

Rory thanked the heavens when he heard the announcement for the pizza concert. That's what the employees called it. He'd made it to stage three of the birthday party.

Reg E. Rat played a less important role for the pizza concert. All the focus was on food and the dumb robot band that would play a bunch of songs while the kids ate.

Rory couldn't go hide backstage. He still had to mingle around the fringes of the party area. He also had to participate in one song, the birthday song. That song came later in the show so Rory had a bit of time to regain his composure.

The arcade session was intense. Kids were trying to pull his tail off. Some of the older kids tried their damnedest to get him to break character. They'd ask him questions, trying to get him to talk but Rory would just nod his giant rat head in a yes or no fashion or if really stumped, he shrugged and turned tail to face another gauntlet of heathen children.

Getting kicked in the shin was par for the course but Rory got booted three times in the arcade. He couldn't appreciate the restraint the Reg E. Rat players before him displayed in order not to beat the crap out of all the godless little children. If he'd gotten slapped, kicked, punched or breathed on funny one more time, he was sure he would lose it.

The pizza concert started in the nick of time.

The children poured out of the arcade faster than water through a break in the levee. Rory found himself basking in the silent cacophony of bells, buzzers, sirens and whistles emanating from the menagerie of the arcade machines.

Skeeball wasn't going to kick him. Alien Invader Attack Z wasn't going to ask him if its father had left it and its mommy. The goofy helicopter bicycle didn't want to get all up on his shit to take a selfie with him. The arcade was his friend.

"Reg E!" Wendy the shift manager shouted, snapping him out of paradise, "pizza concert, now! Mingle! Mingle! Mingle!"

Reg E. Rat slumped his shoulders and padded off back to the birthday party area. His giant rat sneakers sliding along the floor. They were weighed down with the burden of celebrity, unable to lift off the floor.

Reg E. Rat stood in the rear of the party room. The kids' attention was focused on the stage. Three spotlights swept to and fro across the red curtain and the disembodied announcer introduced The World's Most Famous Birthday Band, The Beasts!

The kids screamed and applauded. The curtains parted and revealed the creepiest shit you've ever seen in your life. A third rate, broken down, dusty and tattered robot rock band.

The band launched into their opening song, "Welcome to the Show." It was an obvious rip-off of the more popular song played at a popular toy store, an ode to a lack of creativity, integrity and consumerism.

Rory couldn't believe he worked for this place.

He was thankful all the attention was off him and he watched along with the rest of the kids and their parents. It was odd, he'd seen this act a million times but something about it seemed different viewing it through his rat eyes.

He could hear the whirring and clicking of the robot bands gearworks over the music they were supposedly playing. He knew this band had been playing together for something like thirty years. He knew they were maintained and cobbled together with unique parts.

If a bolt holding an arm to a body broke, the maintenance guy would jam a fork in it and call it fixed. If an eyeball popped out, the maintenance guy would shove a wad of balled-up duct tape in the gaping eye socket and cram the eyeball back into place. That's why several of the band members looked like they were looking in two different directions, taped on eyeballs.

That wasn't even the weirdest part.

The piano player, a gorilla named Cheezy, played the opening notes to the song. The guitar player, a wolf (who was missing one of his eyes) named Pupperoni, slid forward on his mount. His arm strummed his faux instrument out of sync with the music. The band had an alligator drummer known the world over as Saucy Jack. Saucy Jack played drums so well you couldn't see his arms beating on the skins because both of his arms were detached from the motor that made them move up and down. Lucky for him all his tracks were pre-recorded.

The band was fronted by the sexy Crusty Goodness, a sultry skunk diva who was also the object of Reg E. Rat's desire. Reg E. Rat had a thing for skunks apparently. Crusty didn't appear from behind the curtain. Instead, just before the opening line to the song, she lowered from a swing above the stage. That really wowed the kids.

It was Rory's job to act lovestruck when Crusty Goodness was lowered from the ceiling.

Rory piloted his rat suit toward the front of the stage. He held his hands over his rat heart and made a pounding motion on his chest. He hoped this conveyed their love he didn't feel an ounce of for the old broken down skunk robot.

Crusty Goodness ignored Reg E. Rat's affections. She wasn't programmed to acknowledge him. The show was recorded before

CHAPTER 12 | 45

the new love twist was scripted into the birthday parties years later. Corporate wrote that bit in to appeal to the senses of little girls. The demographics of girls' birthday parties were down at the time.

Rory noted all the birthday parties taking place today were for boys. They weren't impressed by the courtship ritual.

The opening song came to an end and Crusty Goodness broke into some stage banter with Pupperoni. It was pablum garbage about how all the kids in the audience looked great. Special mention was given to "the kid over there in the crown," as if there were only one birthday boy in the crowd.

Rory didn't mind. He wasn't supposed to interact with the band during banter since they wouldn't be able to acknowledge him. It wasn't in their programming.

Rory observed from the side of the stage letting them go through their spiel until the next song started and he would have to swoon over Crusty again.

While he stood there, silently mouthing the script, he noticed Pupperoni's jaw begin to get lazy. He wasn't closing his chompers all the way shut as he talked. The more he spoke the more his jaw movement disintegrated into a wiggle.

Rory did his best not to laugh. The robots breaking down in the middle of a performance wasn't anything new. But, to Rory, the technical difficulties Pupperoni was experiencing tickled his funny bone. He fought back a laughing fit in the suit.

Then, he made an impromptu acting decision. He decided that Reg E. Rat should be laughing at the band. They were doing their best to deliver the terrible jokes that were written for them. Why not punch it up and let go the laughter he was holding back anyway.

Reg E. Rat started to snicker. A few of the kids who sat closest to him took their eyes off the show and glanced at Reg E. Rat. They were startled that he made any noise whatsoever. There was a social contract that the kids all knew: Reg E. Rat didn't talk, not making a peep except to say "Rat-Tat-Wa-Hooey," and he only did that from the stage.

The more Rory watched Pupperoni's jaw wiggle limp like he'd

just got a shot of Novocain at the dentist office, the more Rory's giggle devolved into doubled over laughter.

Now all eyes were on Reg E. Rat. He was laughing like a maniac. The parents were beginning to think there was a coked-up drug addict in the suit. Some kids started to panic, knowing the maniacal laughter of a 7-foot-tall rat was not part of the act.

Rory couldn't hold it back. He didn't care. He was certain he was going to get fired. He saw Wendy stomping toward him through the wire mesh of Reg E. Rat's eyes and the tears in his own eyes.

Oh well, fuck this job anyway.

Before the manager could step in and move Reg E. Rat backstage, away from the kids, The Beasts started to play their second song. And when they started, all hell broke loose.

## 13

### THE BURDEN OF THE BEASTS

IF SAUCY JACK were a real live drummer, he would've thought it odd that sparks streamed out of his mouth as the band launched into the second song of the set. But Saucy Jack the Alligator wasn't alive, he was a robot, so he played through the abnormality.

Saucy Jack wasn't the only robot glitching at the start of the second song. Cheezy the Gorilla hit the ivories so hard, he pounded right through them, decimating the faux-piano he'd been playing for the past thirty years.

Pupperoni's jaw unhinged. It would have clanged against the floor but it was stopped just short of hitting the ground by the cadre of wires still attached to it. Now his jaw looked something like an electronic ZZ Top beard.

The malfunctioning robot band caught the attention of all the parents and kids. The sparking, grinding, clacks and clangs were impossible to ignore. However, full on pandemonium didn't ensue until Crusty Goodness, still swinging from her perch, leapt off the swing like a ninja and crashed down on top of Christopher's table.

She stood, autonomous of the cables and wiring that controlled her. Crusty threw her arms to the heavens and screamed like a diva hitting high E three octaves higher than most mortal women.

That's when everyone screamed and scrambled.

Crusty Goodness cackled and kicked the Reg E. Rat birthday pizza (Baked with Crusty Goodness™) off the table. The pie spun through the air and splattered a little girl on the side of the head. She screamed, the magma-hot melted cheese scalding the side of her head. The girl went down, wailing, pulling the cheese off her face. Her attempts were all in vain, the cheese, so ooey-gooey, only pulling in strings and spreading over her face and hands, doing more damage as it took bubbling skin grafts with it.

On stage, Pupperoni ignored his hanging jaw and lifted his knee straight up, dislodging himself from the stage he'd been bolted to for three decades. Electricity arced underfoot as he ripped himself free of everything that tethered him to the ground. He growled because he was a wolf over his robot facade. With the one eye he had remaining, he honed in on a little boy who made a mad dash away from the front of the stage. Pupperoni raised his guitar over his head and jumped off the stage, bringing his fake guitar (made mostly of sheet-metal and wire) down on the kid's head. The little boy's skull caved in like it was a cardboard box filled with styrofoam packing peanuts. The sound his head made sounded roughly the same.

While Crusty Goodness and Pupperoni were mauling the scrambling children, Cheezy stood up from behind his decimated piano. He'd tickled those keys for a third of a century and now that it was destroyed, he had no reason to sit there and not play. For the first time since he was pieced together, he stood up and beat on his chest like... well, like a big gorilla. If Cheezy could have feelings, he'd have felt liberated.

As he pounded his chest, he accidentally punched through his outer covering. He left a big hole where his heart would've been if he'd one. Instead, what he had in that part of his chest was a series of relays and capacitors that received electronic impulses from the The Beasts central control unit located backstage. That cluster of doodads and wires were damaged beyond repair and Cheezy was now autonomous of the central control system. He was free to execute the last command sent to him: KILL.

Cheezy lunged off the stage, running on his feet and knuckles like the primate he was fabricated to resemble. The first victim he honed in on was a mom who huddled over her child, trying to wrangle the little rugrat away from the chaos and toward the exit. Cheezy pounced into the air, feet first and walloped mommy with a critical drop kick.

The mother convulsed on the ground, her spine shattered by the gorilla's vicious attack. Just like Cheezy, her neurons had become disconnected from her central nervous system and her body was convulsing from all the misfiring neurons sending confused electric impulses coursing through her body. Her child lay helpless underneath her as she writhed and smothered the kid to death. She wouldn't have time to mourn; she would expire a moment later.

There was now a log jam trying to press past Reg E. Rat's exit corridor. If not for Reg E. Rat's crack team of security personnel manning the exits, more lives could have been saved. But, as per corporate policy, nobody was allowed to exit the facility until parent and child were matched with the invisible ink code they were stamped with upon entry. That ensured that no kid-touchers could sneak in to Reg E. Rat's and make off with some easy prey. It had been a problem at Reg E. Rat's early on but not anymore.

The orderly exit protocol that was in place was made more chaotic by the eagerness of the parents and children to flee certain death. This only made the security check take that much longer.

Which is why Saucy Jack was having a grand old time playing William Tell up on the stage. Saucy Jack also went rogue from the central control system. He'd fashioned a bow out of the busted up piano and piano wire lying about on stage. He then used his drumsticks as makeshift arrows and was picking off men, women and children in the horde piled-up trying to escape the calamity.

Saucy Jack snickered as he surveyed a number of bodies lying face down on the ground with drumsticks impaled in the backs. The blood that poured out from around the wounds reminded him of the pizza sauce he was the namesake for. How apropos.

The Beasts were enjoying their new gig as a bunch of crazy marauders. They'd been entertainers for so long, playing the same songs, day in and day out to crowds of naive children and disinterested parents. Now they were free of their burden. They were no longer The Beasts; they were *The Maulers*!

# 14

## REG E. AND THE RAT

WENDY YANKED Reg E. Rat backstage. They both heard screaming, pops and crashes from out front. The sounds infuriated Rory's manager. She thought Reg E. Rat breaking character had upset everyone so much that they started a riot.

She swatted Reg E. Rat's head as hard as she could and the head tumbled off Rory's shoulders and rolled on the floor as if he'd been decapitated.

Rory saw right away that the screaming and ruckus wasn't his fault. There was a kid fucking around with The Beasts central controls. He reminded Rory of that kid from the *Toy Story* movie. He clutched two bundles of wires he'd torn loose from the guts of the machine. The controller itself, a large metal panel populated with lights and buttons and switches and readouts, looked like a diabolical contraption straight out of a sixties-era spy thriller (and that's probably when it was manufactured).

The kid cackled, actually fucking cackled, as he shook the wire bundles in his hand. Sparks rained out of the busted access panel where the wiring had been ripped apart. There were several buzzers buzzing and a cadre of red lights blinking in an epileptic fit of urgency. It didn't take a computer engineer to know that there was a major malfunction with Reg E. Rat's Birthday Party Fun Band.

*That's* what all the ruckus is about. The band was doing God-knows-what up on stage and was freaking the kids out. Rory took umbrage with his manager for failing to assess the situation correctly and place the blame on him.

"I take umbrage with you blaming me for what's clearly this shit head's fault!" Rory pointed to the kid who continued his maniacal laughter now that he had an audience to witness his shit-headery.

"We don't refer to the customers as shit heads, Rory! What's gotten into you?"

"You fucking kidding me right now?" Rory said, aghast that he was still being reprimanded.

"Insubordination! You're fired!"

"Oh yeah! Well good, because I quit anyway!" Rory said, pulling off his right Reg E. Rat hand and slapping it across the manager's face like he'd just challenged her to a duel.

The manager stood there, mouth agape, dumbfounded that an employee would dare strike her.

The crazy kid laughed even more. "Ha! This is the best party ever! I get to watch Reg E. Rat kick the shit out of some broad!"

That caught the manager's attention. She reacted like the kid appeared out of thin air. Rory watched as her eyes darted to the boy, the controller, the sparks and the cackling. She rubbed her cheek where the rat hand smacked her as she pieced it all together.

She charged the kid, "You *cannot* be back here. This area is for authorized personnel only! Show me your ID stamp right now so I can bring you back to your parents and tell them what you've done here."

She reached for the kid's arm to detain him. The kid pulled his hand away and slapped her across the other side of her face, harder than Reg E. Rat had before.

The manager screeched, shocked that a child would dare defy her command.

"That's it! You're out of here. No more parties for you. You are permanently banned!" she said, grabbing him by the back of the neck.

The kid pivoted and punched her square in the gut. Rory actually heard the wind rush out of her lungs as he watched Wendy fall to her knees faster than a Catholic begging for forgiveness. Rory was frozen. The tiny, devious part of him had enjoyed watching his former boss get put in her place. The bigger person in him knew he had to stop the kid from beating up his former manager even if she was a corporate shill and lacked a sense of humanity.

Rory stepped up to the kid.

"Stay back, Rat!" the kid said.

"Dude, you hurt her," Rory said.

"And I'm gonna hurt you next if you don't fuck off!"

Rory took another step. The kid was trying to sound menacing but he was still a kid. Rory saw fear behind the veneer of anger.

The kid turned and jammed both of his hands into the sparking guts of the control panel. He clutched another handful of wiring. The frayed ends of the live wires arced and exploded in a brilliant ball of white light. Loud pops punctuated the raw power flowing through the system.

The kid spasmed like he was having a seizure. He was the conduit for massive amounts of electricity coursing through his body.

Rory paused. He smelled barbequed meat.

One final pop filled the room like a stray kernel bursting when all the popcorn had burst. The kid was smoking. He took one step back from the fried control panel.

The boy should've dropped dead. Instead, he turned and faced Rory. His face was blackened and his hands were a giant black ball of melted wiring and exposed, charred flesh. Rory thought they looked like the world's most grotesque boxing gloves.

The kid smiled, holding one of his mutated hands aloft. Spiderwebs of blue lightning erupted in a ball around his smoldering fist.

"Take care of her," he said to no one in particular.

Rory dared not approach the kid any closer. But he also couldn't bring himself to run. He had no idea if he was in a fight or flight situation.

The curtain to the stage parted and a seven-foot-tall robot alligator stepped through. He held what looked like a bow and arrow cobbled together from broken furniture.

"Jesus Christ, its Saucy Jack," Rory whispered in disbelief.

Without hesitation, Saucy Jack mounted a drumstick on his bow and arrow and reared back, aiming at the motionless body of his boss. He let go the string and the drum stick impaled itself into her skull. At that close range, it had no trouble breaking the thick bone encasing her now lifeless brain.

Rory was now certain this was a flight situation. He backed up a few steps then turned to run but ran right into another boy and his dad.

## 15

LIVING THE NIGHTMARE

Mortimer's worst fears came true. That fucking robot band had come to life. He dreamed of this moment for a lifetime. The dreams were nightmares.

When Mortimer was Ichabod's age, he attended his first birthday party at Reg E. Rat's Birthday Fun Center. The party was for a girl in his class, Christine. Mortimer was in love with Christine. When he looked at Christine his stomach would tighten and his heart would erupt in flames.

Reg E. Rat's Fun Center was new back then. It had recently opened and Christine was the envy of every kid in class. The place was immaculate. The video games were state of the art for the time. And the pizza, well, the pizza was still awful. But it didn't matter back then. Reg E. Rat's wasn't about pizza. Reg E. Rat's was paradise for kids. Nobody gave a shit about the pizza.

Mortimer remembered Christine's party like it happened yesterday. Everything in Reg E. Rat's was polished and shiny. The games all functioned perfectly. All the employees were the kind of happy normally reserved for Disney World. The band was plush and colorful. They sounded and looked like state of the art animatronics.

Mortimer sat across from Christine. He was able to soak in her beauty the entire party. When it was time to play video games, she split off with her girlfriends but Mortimer stuck close to her, never letting her out of his sight. Then it was back to the tables for pizza and entertainment.

The party hostess came out and did the same spiel that was recited thirty years later at Christopher's party, only with genuine enthusiasm. The curtains parted and The Beasts began the show. Their mouths and arms and legs all moved in perfect time with the music. Their eyes blinked in unison. They were brilliant.

During The Beasts' final song, Christine was invited on stage. She was lucky, like a special charm. She got to be *on the stage* at Reg E. Rat's. Crusty Goodness sang the last song just for the birthday girl. It was magical.

When the song was over and the show ended, Christine was ushered backstage to receive her super special birthday present from Reg E. Rat himself. Mortimer applauded with the rest of the children. He was so happy for Christine. Such a special girl deserved a special present.

He couldn't wait for Christine to return from backstage so he could see how awesome the special present from Reg E. Rat would be. It had to be glorious. Maybe it would be a real, live pony or something. Reg E. Rat must have tons of pony friends he could give away to all the special birthday kids who came to his Fun Center.

The pizza was served. The juice was poured. The kids all got lost in the hub-bub of Reg E. Rat's.

But Mortimer grew worried. Christine never came back. She didn't get to eat any pizza.

Then, the party hostess started to serve cake. Christine never got to eat the first piece.

Mortimer thought it was bananas that nobody seemed to notice. The kids were all invited to play more video games when they finished their cake. Mortimer lingered, waiting for Christine. He was the last kid sitting at the table in front of the stage. He didn't even see Christine's parents.

Mortimer's dad told him it was time to go. Reg E. Rat's had cleared out, and he was one of the last kids there.

"What happened to Christine?" Mortimer asked, looking at the stage, willing her to come back.

"I dunno, Mort. Maybe she got sick? Maybe she had to leave early?"

"Maybe." Mortimer didn't like that answer. It didn't sound right.

Mortimer left the party. He looked back one last time, hoping against hope that he would see Christine come from behind the curtain riding her pony. Instead he saw the maintenance guy sweeping the stage. His broom pushed the curtain aside and he would swear for the rest of his life he saw Christine's head clamped in the alligator's jaws.

He never stepped a foot in Reg E. Rat's again.

Until he was forced to take his son to Christopher's party.

He'd spent thirty years convincing himself that what he thought he saw was just a horrifying memory he'd built up in his imagination to explain why he never saw Christine again. But his first visit since that day only proved what he saw that day was real.

The Beasts were child-killing maniacs. After thirty years they no longer felt the need to hide their diabolical nature. Reg E. Rat's was a place to sacrifice children to the angry robot demons disguised as a Birthday Party Fun Center.

Mortimer corralled Ichabod when the robots attacked. He dragged his son toward the front door but that exit was already log jammed. He saw bodies fall around him. He wasn't going to keep his son in the horde and wait to get picked off. He needed to find another way out.

If the front door wasn't a good way out, then he had to head for the back door. He remembered seeing *Authorized Staff Only* doors when he went to the bathroom. One of those had to access the back door.

He dragged Ichabod the opposite direction that everyone else fled.

The first door they came to was marked *Backstage Area*. Mortimer tried the knob and it opened. He ushered Ichabod inside and ran in behind him. Then a giant rat with a human head barreled into the two of them and all three crumpled in a pile on the floor.

The guy in the Reg E. Rat costume looked at Mortimer as if he'd appeared out of thin air. Then his eyes widened and he said, "Run! Run!" and used Mortimer's chest to push himself back up to his feet. Instead of running, the rat guy picked Ichabod and Mortimer up by their arms.

The rat guy ran out the door. Mortimer watched him flee then scanned the room. He looked behind him to see what the rat guy fled from. He was met with a blinding smash to the gut. Something exploded in his body. He went limp and crumpled back to the floor.

He didn't blackout, but the pain crippled him. It was the worst pain he'd experienced in his abdomen, now magnified a hundred times.

He heard his son say, "Marker! Holy shit," which sounded like he was underwater when he said it. Mortimer made a mental note to give Ichabod a stern lesson on using foul language.

Mortimer looked up at the dark ceiling. It was twisting, spinning, stretching. He tried to regain focus. He heard more yelling, garbled. A foot stepped on his chest. He thought his stomach would explode from the massive pressure. He thought maybe whoever hit him was chasing his son.

Mortimer didn't like that idea. He tried like hell to clear his head. Focus. Stop the room from spiraling away from his body. He knew he needed to get up and help his son. He needed to stop whoever hit him and was going after now.

And why had Ichabod cursed at a marker?

## 16

FLIGHT OF THE ICKY

"Mark R! Holy shit!" Ichabod shocked himself when the s-word flew out of his mouth. He took his eyes off Mark R. and looked at his dad, not sure who would hurt him worse. His dad was out of it, laying on the floor, staring up at nothing. He needed to get Mark R. away from his father so he couldn't hurt him anymore.

Mark R. wore strange boxing gloves. Blue sparks orbited the misshapen gloves. He reminded Ichabod of the emperor from Star Wars who used lightning as his weapon against good.

Mark R. set his sights on Ichabod. "Get over here, Icky Sticky! Now!"

"No! Get away from my dad!"

"Sticky Icky Sticky Icky Icky,"

"Shut up!"

"You're dead, Icky Sticky!"

Ichabod ran. He ran because he had to. He ran because it would get Mark R. away from his dad. He ran because this birthday party suddenly sucked.

Ichabod had no idea where to run to safety. He could have gone right out the backstage door and headed down a dark hallway, but he didn't know what lay down that path. He stuck with what he knew and ran back into the party room.

It looked like a war zone. There were bodies everywhere, kids and adults. He didn't focus on them, he ran over and around them like they were obstacles in gym class. The exit was plugged up with a massacre of bodies. He saw two of the crazy robots attacking people as they pushed to get out of the party.

There was a scream and he saw a decapitated head launch out of the melee. He thought it looked like that kid, Johnny Macchio from Mrs. Bledsoe's class across the hall. Ichabod remembered he was good at basketball in gym class. Now, his head could be used for a ball.

Icky had no clue where to run. He headed for the arcade. He glanced over his shoulder. Mark R. stomped at him. He wasn't running but walked like a sasquatch toward Ichabod. Mark R. knew as well as Icky that he could run all he wanted but he wasn't going to get away.

Icky ran around a maze of arcade games looking for something to get Mark R. off his ass. Down the end of the aisle he saw his salvation. A helicopter. He beat feet as fast as he could; he'd need all the time he could buy to get the thing up in the air.

The helicopter was a stupid little kid ride. In happier times (like half an hour ago) Ichabod desperately wanted to ride the helicopter but he knew it was a little kid ride and he knew everyone would tease him for the rest of his life for taking it for a spin. It was a single seat thing, not much different from those mechanical horses or cars that you would plunk a quarter into and it would sway back and forth for a few minutes. But the helicopter ride at Reg E. Rat's worked by straddling the helicopter body and putting your feet on the bicycle pedals it was equipped with. The faster you pedaled the faster it rose up into the air. It would go about eight feet up in the air too.

Ichabod pedaled like he was on the final stretch of the Tour de France. He rose into the air as he watched Mark R. bear down on the helicopter. Mark R. jumped, leading with his boxing glove zapper but Ichabod rose just out of reach and Mark R. crashed to the ground.

Ichabod laughed. He triumphed. He wanted to yell down, "Fuck you, Mark R!" but he dared not in case his dad had gotten up and come to look for him.

Ichabod stopped pedaling. The helicopter began to descend. He'd dropped several feet before he realized what was happening. Watching Mark R. get to his knees inspired him to pedal again. Icky realized he was going to have to pedal, pedal, pedal and keep pedaling if he was going to keep himself out of reach.

Mark R. got to his feet. He saw Ichabod's dilemma as well. "You can't keep pedaling forever, Icky Sticky! I'm gonna wait here and kick your ass when your legs give out."

Ichabod pedaled hard. Too hard, he would tucker himself sooner rather than later. The fear clouded his ability to realize he only needed to keep the pedals moving to stay up, pedaling harder or faster didn't do anything other than tire him out faster.

Ichabod needed another escape plan. He thought he foiled Mark R. but he only managed to corner himself.

From his vantage point he could see all around Reg E. Rat's Birthday Fun Center. He watched as the Cheezy the gorilla robot tore somebody's mother's arms off her body. The mom screamed like she was in a horror movie. Even the blood that blasted out of her shoulder stumps looked like bad special effects he'd seen when he snuck in watching a late night horror movie on cable after his mom and dad had gone to bed.

Icky knew those robots were maiming and killing everyone who came within their grasp. Ichabod thought maybe if he was able to draw the attention of one of The Beasts to him, they would have to go through Mark R first. Of course, he'd then have to deal with the killer robot himself but at least he would get Mark R. out of the picture. That might be preferable.

"Hey, Cheezy! Ya dumb ape! Over here!" Ichabod waved his

hands over his head doing everything he could to be loud and observable.

"You are so stupid, Icky Sticky. They won't help you; they'll kill you. Oh well, whatever. If they don't, I will," Mark R. called up to him.

Ichabod made weird noises like, *"WOODLE, WOODLE, WOODLE! YIP! YIP! AYEEEEEEE!"* to draw the gorilla's attention.

Cheezy, the gorilla robot, was focused on rearranging the mother's body parts. Laser focused like, well, like a robot carrying out a command. It would not be shook until it completed its task.

Other kids, however, did take notice of Ichabod up on the helicopter. They saw a friend who found a safe space. In a panic, several of them ran toward the helicopter.

Mark R. sneered when he saw the cavalry arrive. More victims.

Ichabod watched from above as a half dozen of his classmates found themselves face to face with Mark R. The bully raised his weird fist to the air. It crackled and hummed with blue electricity. He saw Cheezy the Gorilla halt the mommy maiming he carried out and walked toward Mark R.

"Oh no!" Ichabod said. He figured it out: somehow Mark R. was controlling The Beasts with those weird gloves he wore.

"Run! Run! Run! The Gorilla is coming!" Ichabod warned his friends.

The kids ran in a pack, not sure which way the threat came for them but knowing that running at Mark R. was a bad idea also. They headed to their left into the maze of arcade games.

Ichabod lost sight of his friends. At least they chose not to run toward Cheezy, who continued to stomp toward Mark R.

The robot gorilla strode up to Mark R. and halted. Mark R. didn't say a word but Cheezy looked like he acknowledged a command and stepped up to the base of the helicopter.

Ichabod's legs were burning up. He didn't think he could keep pedaling much longer. The massive robot gorilla below gave him a little extra incentive to fight through the ache he felt in his thighs.

Cheezy grabbed hold of the pedestal the helicopter was mounted atop. The robot started to shake the whole contraption. Ichabod hung on for dear life. He wouldn't have to worry about pedaling; the robot was going to shake him out of the helicopter.

"Now that's a cool ride!" Mark R. jeered from below. "Shake it harder," he commanded Cheezy.

Cheezy did as he was instructed.

Ichabod gripped the handles as he was jostled back and forth. The gorilla rocked the ride so hard he felt like a coconut being shook loose from a palm tree.

Cheezy wasn't programmed to calculate the physics of things. He couldn't estimate the center of gravity, trajectories and the effects of force on mass. All he knew was to shake the ride harder as he was instructed. The helicopter made the whole contraption top heavy and soon, he swayed too far and the whole ride fell past its stability point.

Ichabod felt the odd sensation of falling. Instinct made him hold tight to the helicopter. It happened fast but it felt like he was tipping over in slow motion. The shaft of the helicopter crashed along the top of a row of arcade machines and stopped the helicopter from smashing into the ground. The sudden stop threw Ichabod off the helicopter and onto the floor. The landing knocked the wind out of him but he was lucky the arcade games stopped the ride from slamming him straight into the ground.

Ichabod fought to suck air back into his lungs. That was the worst feeling in the world.

He was scooped up off the floor by his friends who'd fled the gorilla. Ichabod was able to grab a breath when he was uprighted.

His six friends encircled him waiting for him to say he was alright.

Ichabod breathed in short fast breaths, building back the oxygen in his body.

He sucked in a long breath and said, "We have to fight back. It's the only way out."

## 17

PREP THE PATIENT FOR SURGERY

Mortimer couldn't move. The pain was searing in his abdomen. He cried. It was the only thing he could do even though sobbing made the pain worse.

He was alone. Nobody would come for him or save his son. They were all trying to save themselves. He never should've brought Ichabod to Reg E. Rat's. He should've followed his gut. Now his gut had exploded and he'd die inside Reg E. Rat's Birthday Fun Center.

He heard the door creek open.

Mortimer wasn't sure if he should call out for help or stay quiet. Was it a kid or parent also looking for refuge backstage? What if one of those monster robots came to put him down for good?

He heard approaching footsteps. They were kind of clunky sounding. Feet too big to be human. That was it. Was it the wolf, the alligator or the gorilla? Maybe it was the skunk diva. Mortimer said a prayer for a swift end and salvation for his son.

The footsteps stopped at his head. Mortimer kept his eyes shut, waiting for the final blow.

It felt like hours but nothing came.

He dared to open his eyes, expecting to see the hammer fall as he did. Instead he looked up at a clown looking back down at him.

"What the —" Mortimer had no way to quantify why he was looking at a clown. Was he already dead? Was God a clown?

"Hey guy," the clown said when he opened his eyes, "we gotta prep you for surgery, stat!"

More foot clomping came through the door. Two more clowns appeared at Mortimer's side. They carried one of those stretchers you see clowns use when they do a rescue routine, just white canvas between two poles.

The clowns lifted Mortimer onto the stretcher. He screamed out in pain. He almost blacked out and was pretty sure he peed himself. He felt fire in his groin.

"Get him to the outpatient care facility! Stat!" The first clown instructed.

The clowns marched Mortimer out of the backstage area. They jogged him down the back hallway. The jostling irritated his blazing innards. Mortimer wanted to beg them to slow down and take it easy but the pain searing through him wouldn't allow him a moment to speak.

The first clown jogged down the hall next to him. He kept yelling, "Stat!" for no particular reason.

There were a few turns left and right and all of a sudden the dimly lit hallway gave way to a room with bright white light. The clowns dropped the stretcher on an examination table. That caused Mortimer a great deal more pain.

So much pain that he finally blacked out as a bright white lamp was shoved in front of his face before he went unconscious.

Mortimer blinked his eyes open. He thought he passed out but he was looking back up at that bright light shining in his face.

The clown stuck his face in between the light and Mortimer's face, "Oh! Looks like the anesthesia has worn off. More drugs, stat!"

Mortimer stared at the clown. Why was there a clown? Why did he have a fondness for the word stat? He was a pretty basic looking clown. He had a white face, red nose, red painted-on smile, big blue happy eyes and curly neon green hair. He wore a white lab coat. It made him look like a doctor clown.

The clown kept staring down at Mortimer. His smile never broke.

"Hey, guy! We're gonna knock you back out, stat. Don't you worry!" He brought a brass horn out of the lab coat of his pocket and squeezed off a honk.

"What's wrong with me?"

"Kidney stones, guy! We're going to remove them, stat! They've punctured your kidney."

"It doesn't hurt anymore."

"Because your kidneys aren't there any more, guy. We got 'em on ice, stat!" The clown tooted his horn again.

Doctor clown nodded to a table next to Mortimer. Mortimer turned his head and saw both of his kidneys in a stainless steel bowl. They weren't resting in a bath of ice but on a bed of lettuce. Both kidneys were severed open with disgusting looking brown pulp oozing out and gnarly looking crystal rocks.

"Is that the kidney stones coming out of them?"

"Oh yeah. Those things are big. Biggest I've ever seen, guy. We're going to get them down to the lab, stat!"

"Why are my kidneys sitting in a bowl of lettuce?"

"They are going to make a great salad, buddy. The guests will eat them up stat!"

"What?"

"Here comes the anesthesia, guy. We'll have you fixed up stat!"

Mortimer blacked out looking at his kidneys sitting in a bowl of lettuce.

Mortimer heard the clown's horn honk before he conked out again.

## 18

BARRICADE

The first police officer arrived at Reg E. Rat's Birthday Party Fun Center about ten minutes after the initial birthday boy was killed.

Officer Brady O'Grady pulled his cruiser along the curb. The call had come in as a Riot-in-Progress. Officer O'Grady chuckled at the use of the word 'riot' at a Reg E. Rat's. What happened, some indignant mother slapped a kid because he wouldn't get the manager? He thought the riot would be as ridiculous as Reg E. Rat's itself.

You could imagine Officer O'Grady's surprise when he strode into the front foyer and was greeted with a bloody human head throw at his chest like he'd just walked onto the court of a pick-up basketball game down at the park. The officer didn't realize what it was until he pulled the head back from his chest and saw that it was a guy he knew from the PBA bowling league.

He dropped Chip Dunwich's head. Officer O'Grady began panting like an overheated dog, looking down into the dead eyes of a guy he'd watched bowl a 291 one cold November evening, two years prior. Poor Dunwich choked hard on a perfect game, clipping off only one pin on the final ball. Still, it was a sight to see.

Chip's bloody, dismembered head was also a sight to see. This was no irate customer displeased with how her child's birthday party was handled. Everything about this call was understated.

"Riot my ass!" Officer O'Grady drew his service revolver.

He took a defensive crouch and duck-walked to the next set of doors. The glass pane shattered. Sharp shards of glass rained down over the floor. O'Grady saw bodies strewn about on the other side of the door. Lots of bodies.

He choked up when he noticed a child's corpse under the lifeless body of his presumed parent. O'Grady stuttered when he keyed his shoulder mic to call for immediate backup.

"Repeat, 91," the dispatcher said, not understanding the words O'Grady mumbled over the airwaves.

"Dispatch. Need immediate backup to Reg E. Rat's. There's a... situation here."

"Situation?" This dispatcher asked, not understanding O'Grady breaking protocol and needing clarification.

"Send more cops and ambulances! There's bodies everywhere!"

"Shit!" the dispatcher said, breaking protocol herself. "Right away, Brady."

O'Grady crouched and waddled through the door. He couldn't believe the number of bodies, so many of them kids. The scene was ghastly. The bodies were mutilated. Limbs were torn off almost all the bodies he saw, adults and children alike. What kind of monster was at work here? What was he up against?

The answer came in the form of a drumstick that zipped through the air and speared him in the leg. Officer O'Grady dropped to his ass, the unexpected pain knocking him off balance. The glass on the ground tore into his ass cheeks. More pain.

O'Grady braced himself with his palms, pushing his ass off the ground but ripping open his hands on glass and dropping his revolver in the process. He skittered away from the glass and took cover behind the hostess podium.

The officer, frantic, felt around his utility belt for his baton. He needed *something* to defend himself from...

He had no idea what he was up against. He still hadn't seen a single assailant. There had to be a whole group. Carnage like this wasn't caused by one upset mother. No way. This was terrorism.

O'Grady felt his baton. His palms screamed when he wrapped his hand around the handle. He fought through the searing pain; it was better than being weaponless. He withdrew the baton from its holster loop and dared to take a peek around the podium.

He was punched square in the face by a giant gorilla fist.

Officer O'Grady's lights went out, but not for good.

The good officer lay unconscious behind the hostess podium, knocked out from a vicious jab from Cheezy the Gorilla. It was a good thing for Officer O'Grady that he was blacked out. He never felt the killer robot gorilla's massive foot stomp his head flat. The red gush that exploded out looked just like the ripe, red inner flesh of a watermelon.

Cheezy turned his attention back toward a pocket of kids who were scampering about the arcade. Saucy Jack moved off the stage and picked up several bodies, holding them under his arm like he was carrying dirty laundry.

Saucy Jack threw the pile of bodies he amassed at the front door to Reg E. Rat's. He gathered up several more bodies and repeated the process. There were plenty of bodies for him to stack up in that manner. Before long, the front doors to Reg E. Rat's Birthday Fun Center was barricaded with a beaver's dam of corpses.

The back-up cops wouldn't be getting through anytime soon.

# 19

## GENERAL ICHABOD

"How are we going to fight a bunch of robots, Icky? I watched Pupperoni kill Sean's mom!" Gerald pronounced mom like, 'mawm.'

Gerald sat next Ichabod in class. Ichabod liked Gerald even though Gerald liked to look over his shoulder to get answers he didn't know when they took tests. Gerald would sit next to him at lunch after taking a test and share his snack with Ichabod as a thank you. Ichabod appreciated the quid pro quo.

"You're right Ger, we can't fight the robots. We have to fight Mark R. He's the one controlling the robots."

Albert, who was always cool enough to pick Ichabod for his team in gym class, said, "I think I'd rather try to fight the robots instead of Mark R."

"I know you don't mean that but yeah, we've gotta stand up to Mark R. It's the only way to stop the robots. He is controlling them."

"Those weird gloves though," Alicia said. Ichabod thought Alicia was the prettiest girl in class even though he told everyone at recess that she was the girl with the most cooties.

Ichabod smiled at her. His heart thumped when she smiled back.

"Yeah, those electric gloves he's wearing are somehow controlling the robots. I saw him use them to command Cheezy to topple the helicopter out of the sky."

Alicia blushed. She was impressed that Icky survived a helicopter crash.

"If we have to fight Mark R. we're going to need weapons!" Herb said. Herb was the kid in class who always had a copy of his dad's old *Soldier of Fortune* magazines in his backpack. His parents had been sending him to karate class since he was in kindergarten. They knew naming their son Herb would require him to take self-defense classes.

If you hung out with Herb after school he was always practicing with a pair of nunchucks his uncle had given him for his birthday last year. Everyone was a little scared of Herb but were glad to have him on their side. Ichabod was glad Herb was on his side today.

"Where do we find weapons in a Reg E. Rat's?" Gerald asked, "There's a sign right at the front entrance that says no guns allowed."

"There's knives in the kitchen, isn't there?" Diz asked and giggled.

The sixth soldier in Ichabod's impromptu army was Diz. Diz's real name was Liz but she was kinda airy. She laughed at everything. She didn't pay a lot of attention to what was going on around her. She just liked being around people. So she got nicknamed Dizzy or Diz instead of Liz. Diz didn't care as long as she was having fun with other kids.

"Brilliant, Diz!" Ichabod said. "Ok Herb. Did you bring your nunchucks?"

"Nope but we can poke around the kitchen. I'm sure there's more than just knives we can use."

They heard the telltale thumping of an approaching robot.

"C'mon, let's go find some stuff to kick Mark R.'s ass!" Icky felt good being a badass.

Ichabod's army smiled. Icky never cursed. They knew he meant business now that he dropped the A-Bomb. That's what leaders are made of.

Ichabod led his band of soldiers away from the thumping footfalls of an approaching robot and toward the hallway where the backstage door and bathrooms were located. He figured access to the kitchen would also be down that hallway since he saw the staff bringing out pizzas from that hall. He also hoped he would run into his dad and find that he was okay.

They clung to the walls where they could keep a low profile. All around them they heard the screams of the injured, cries for help and the whir of servo motors driving the robot rampage.

They found the hallway slunk into the shadows of the dim lit corridor.

Ichabod opened the first door they came upon.

Gerald said, "Icky, that says backstage. Not the kitchen."

"I know," Ichabod said, peering in and finding the room empty. His heart sank. "I thought maybe I'd find something in here." His dad was gone. He didn't know if that was good or bad. He sided on the side of hope.

He backed out of the room and led them further down the hall.

There was a door marked *Management Only* and then another marked *Kitchen Staff Only*. Bingo!

The door to the kitchen was one of those doors that swing in or out to make entry and exit easy for staff carrying hot pizza and dirty dishes.

Ichabod pushed the door in, they all huddled over one another to peek inside. They didn't hear the clanking of pots or pans. They didn't hear running water, washing dishes or orders being barked out. Not even the sizzle of grease frying up French fries.

Ichabod motioned the group to proceed into the kitchen.

He indicated for them to split up and look around with his hands. He wanted to make as little noise as possible in case a cook or someone was around.

Herb found a big chef's knife right away. He brandished it to let everyone know he'd found a weapon.

Diz found a pizza cutter. It wasn't the rolling wheel kind but a half-moon of stainless steel with a wooden handle along the flat end. You could place it across a whole pizza pie, rock it back and forth to make a single cut through the whole thing. It looked like it could cut open a neck in one fell swoop as well. Diz danced with her new toy.

"I'm using this pizza shovel!" Albert declared. The pizza shovel, as he called it, was the giant spatula with the long handle you use to retrieve the pizza pies out of the ovens. Ichabod wasn't sure it was heavy enough to cause much damage but it was big and wieldy and could be intimidating if nothing else.

Alicia still scrambled around looking for something to use. She passed over knives, spatulas, pizza cutters and instead found a metal bottle the size of a fire extinguisher. She grinned. "I'm using *this*," she cackled and pressed the button on the nozzle on top of the bottle. A wicked blue flame jetting out the business end.

All their eyes lit up. "Whoa! Cool!" Diz said.

Ichabod grabbed two frying pans, handing one to Gerald. "Okay, we're all equipped. Now we have to find Mark R."

They heard the thud of robot footsteps approach outside the kitchen door.

"Sounds like Mark R. found us first," Ichabod said.

The kitchen door blew off its hinges into the kitchen. Debris rained down everywhere. The kids all ducked for cover.

Pupperoni ducked through the doorway, his jaw dragging along the floor.

## 20

### THE FIXINGS BAR

Mortimer opened his eyes. His kidneys were gone. Instead, he looked at his arm lying stretched out next to him, strapped down next to the operating table he was lying on.

"Hey, guy!" the clown giggled. "Got you all fixed up. But we've got some elective surgery to do, stat!"

"Elective surgery? I didn't elect for any of this surgery!" Mortimer said, his voice quivering.

He'd gone from the depths of Hell to whatever lay underneath. He wished he were back at Reg E. Rat's. In fact, he wasn't so sure he wasn't *still* in Reg E. Rat's. He didn't recall an ambulance ride to this so-called surgery center.

"Don't you feel better, stat?" Dr. Clown asked him.

Mortimer thought that was a stupid question. How could he feel better when he was strapped down to a table, being treated like a science experiment. Of course he didn't feel—

Actually, he did feel better. Now that Dr. Clown mentioned it, the severe discomfort he'd been feeling for a week was gone. He felt no pressure, no cramping, no searing pain. The worst pain he'd experienced in his entire life was gone.

Realizing that, Mortimer felt great!

"I do. I do feel better!"

"Stat?"

"Stat," Mortimer said, not knowing what Dr. Clown meant by that but, screw it, Mortimer felt great. He felt like he should jump up and explode into song like this was the big scene to the end of act two of this maniac musical he'd been immersed in all day.

Dr. Clown threw his hands in the air. "Stat!"

Mortimer wanted to throw his hands in the air with Dr. Clown. He wanted to hug him and prance around. Instead, he gave Dr. Clown another triumphant, "Stat!"

Dr. Clown's smile turned sinister. He placed his triumphant white-gloved clown hands down on Mortimer's restrained arm. "Now we start elective surgery. Stat."

Fuck it, Mortimer thought. The clown can do all the surgery on me he'd like. "I elect to have the surgery! Have at it, Dr. Clown! Stat!"

Dr. Clown lifted a surgical instrument off a tray nearby. It was so shiny. It looked like a meat cleaver, but it was silver and polished to a mirror finish. It looked like it could slice through granite.

Dr. Clown plucked off a red nylon hair from his clown wig. He squinted an eye and lined the tip of the hair up to the edge of the clever. He brought the hair to the sharpened edge. Mortimer watched, fascinated, as the blade split the fine hair split in two. That sucker was sharp!

"Wow, Doc! You're going to fix me right up with that bad boy. Say what kind of procedure have I elected for anyway?"

"Pepperoni. Stat."

Pepperoni? Mortimer liked pepperoni. He never heard of such treatment but if the doc was going to slice up some pepperoni with that clever and feed it to him, Mortimer was all in. This is the best surgery center ever!

Dr. Clown grasped Mortimer's hand and brought the clever up

over his head. A nurse clown scampered into the operating room with a violin. She stood over Dr. Clown and Mortimer and played that *Ree! Ree! Ree!* sound from *Psycho*. She high-stepped, on the double, out of the room. Her oversized clown shoes slapped on the floor which Mortimer found hysterical.

Dr. Clown brought the meat cleaver down on Mortimer's wrist.

Now Mortimer had one less hand than he did just a moment ago. Mortimer didn't know how that was going to make him feel better. It didn't hurt much. The cut was so clean. Mortimer was impressed.

Dr. Clown put down the meat cleaver. The blood splatter looked awesome against the polished mirror surface of the blade.

He rolled his instrument tray out of the way and rolled an electric meat slicer into Mortimer's view.

"Whatcha gonna do with that?" Mortimer asked through his dopey smile.

To answer Mortimer, Dr. Clown flipped a switch and the blade began to spin. Dr. Clown grabbed hold of Mortimer's handless arm and placed it on the meat slicer. "Pepperoni time!"

"Stat," Mortimer reminded him.

"Stat," Dr. Clown said.

Dr. Clown steadied Mortimer's arm and pushed the tray of the meat slicer toward the blade with the other. The instrument cut through Mortimer's arm like it was soft butter. A paper-thin slice fell to a tray staged at the back of the slicer.

Dr. Clown held up the slice to the light. He nodded, satisfied.

"Whoa! I've got a pepperoni arm!" It felt to Mortimer like he was at the dentist. Everything was so funny and jolly, including watching a clown with questionable credentials slice his arm into pepperoni.

"Pepperoni, stat!" Dr. Clown said and went back to work on Mortimer's arm.

Mortimer watched as Dr. Clown methodically rode his arm back and forth across the meat slicer. He overlapped the slices in rows on the holding tray. When his arm was sliced down just shy of his elbow, Dr. Clown turned the meat slicer off.

The nurse approached once more. Mortimer heard her giant clown shoes slapping as she approached. She retrieved the tray of arm pepperoni.

"To the kitchen, stat!" Dr. Clown instructed Nurse Clown. Nurse Clown saluted him and slapped her way out of the room again.

"That's enough pepperoni?" Mortimer asked.

"Enough pepperoni!" Dr. Clown said. "Now the sausage, stat!"

Dr. Clown pulled out a stainless steel canister. He depressed a button on the nozzle and a blue jet of flame hissed to life. He took the flame to the end of Mortimer's sliced up arm and seared the meat closed.

Very sterile, Mortimer thought, pleased with the level of care he was receiving at the surgery center.

Dr. Clown moved to Mortimer's leg. "Sausage, stat!"

## 21

### FOOD FIGHT

Pupperoni stalked the kitchen per the instructions he received in his circuitry. He was unable to communicate the status of his mission back to the command center. His jaw, a vital part of his commlink, was disabled and dragged along the floor.

Pupperoni didn't need two-way communication to execute his orders. He had one ocular circuit still working which meant he could see but his depth of vision was limited with the other ocular circuit long ago replaced with a ping pong ball. As long as he could see, he could kill.

Limited sensory data feeding his processor indicated the targets were in this quadrant. Initial scouting of the area revealed no targets in sight. There was a conflict of data. His programming directed him to conduct a more intensive search.

He moved around the quadrant, scanning for targets.

Pupperoni's old servo motors, that drove his movements, buzzed as he walked. A trained electrician would've recognized the sound of circuits shorting out. The robot was not designed to work free of its wiring harness that drove him for so long on the stage. Pupperoni, the guitar playing wolf, was unaware of his slow death.

Pupperoni was also not a trained soldier. He only knew stalk and kill. He walked past Alicia, who was hiding under a prep table. She held her breath, not daring to make the slightest sound.

Albert tucked himself away in the dry goods pantry. Pupperoni moved past him, unknowing.

Diz and Gerald stowed away in the walk-in freezer. Pupperoni didn't bother to check any doors. He walked right past.

Herb chose to hide behind the pizza oven. If you could call it hiding. It was almost as if he wanted to be found. Pupperoni walked past the mouth of the pizza oven, which had a chain conveyor that crept through the oven at a snail's pace. The movement was timed to process a pizza through it to cook the tasteless, cardboard-like food things that, visually, looked like pizza pies. Pupperoni found Herb at the back end of the oven.

Pupperoni's old circuitry made him slow. What he lacked in speed he made up for in power. The robot reared back its arm to strike the kid. The kid was designed for speed. Pupperoni's ocular sensor went dead when the kid jammed a knife into his one good eye socket. The robot continued through with its punch but, blinded, missed the target.

Pupperoni now began to swing both of his fists. He couldn't see. All he could do was throw punches and hope one of them might land on the target.

The target had moved behind the Pupperoni. The robot kept throwing punches at nothing. It rotated forty five degrees and threw several more punches. When nothing landed, he turned again and threw another set of test punches.

He didn't see the other kids come out of hiding. Herb kept himself at Pupperoni's back. He looked for a weakness to exploit. It was going to be hard to cut a metal robot to pieces with a chef knife.

The robot pivoted again and Herb moved with it. The kid was between the robot and the pizza oven. He felt heat radiating from the oven.

Herb motioned the others to come closer. He was going to need them to lead Pupperoni where he wanted him. Herb directed the others to stand by the front of the pizza oven. He utilized hand signals to remain quiet.

Pupperoni continued to throw fruitless punches.

Herb motioned for the others to make noise.

He saw Ichabod raise an eyebrow. Ichabod knew making noise would draw the robot to them. Herb threw out his hands to silently say. "C'mon! Trust me."

The others looked to Ichabod. He nodded, reluctantly.

Ichabod started clapping.

Pupperoni froze. His circuits recalculated the location of the target. He stomped toward the clapping.

Ichabod's eyes widened. He didn't know what the plan was beyond luring Pupperoni toward him and the others. He looked to Herb, shrugged his shoulders, asking silently if he should fight or flee?

Herb, crept behind Pupperoni, he pointed at the oven.

Ichabod didn't understand. Was Herb telling him to hide in the oven? Didn't he realize the thing was lit and would toast them to a crisp before Pupperoni had the chance?

Herb saw Ichabod's confusion. He motioned for Ichabod to stay put, don't run. He hoped Ichabod would hold his ground, he'd need Ichabod and the others to help him with what was to come next.

Alicia tugged on Ichabod's shirt. The others stopped clapping. Only Ichabod continued. He turned his head to look at the others and mouthed the word, "Stay!"

They looked ready to bail. Pupperoni couldn't see them. A few more steps and he'd be able to clobber them all with one punch.

Herb ran past Pupperoni and stood with the group.

Pupperoni reared back his metal fist, estimating he was within striking distance of the source of the clapping.

"Push!" Herb yelled and crouched and sprang low at Pupperoni's hip.

The others rammed in behind Herb. They plowed into

Pupperoni like seven tiny linebackers pushing through one giant defenseman. Pupperoni's servos struggled to switch gears and regain balance.

They heard the robot's drive motor whine as they shoved him toward the mouth of the oven. The robot twisted as it fell backward and slammed hard against the chain that pulled the pizzas through the oven. The wires that dangled from Pupperoni's dislodged jaw got tangled into the chain mesh and started to pull Pupperoni's Jaw into the oven. The wires spooled into the chain like fishing line on a reel.

The kids all stepped back and watched Pupperoni struggle to loosen his jaw from the oven. The one part of his equipment that had held up all these years and never needed replacement was going to be the end of him.

The wiring strung out of Pupperoni's mouth and into the oven. Pupperoni fought back but the wiring wouldn't snap. The kids all watched in shock as Pupperoni's head was drawn into the mouth of the oven.

Sure, he was a robot, but he acted like a living thing and the kids were terrified to watch something die a slow death.

Ichabod knew they had to watch and get hardened against this cruel world. Childhood was over. They'd have to take out others to save themselves. Including Mark R.

Pupperoni was dragged deeper into the oven, flames flared out of its mouth like a fire spitting demon. Fueled by melting rubber and scorched metal, the heat in the oven became overbearing.

"Ugh," Steve wrinkled his nose as black smoke whistled out of the mouth of the pizza oven, "that smells awful."

"That's all the robots' innards melting. All the plastic coating, the wire and the copper wiring. It's not healthy to breathe in. Let's get out of here," Ichabod recommended.

The others coughed, choking on the fumes. They were hesitant to move. They watched, savoring the victory. They'd overcome and destroyed one of the killer robots. Their squad could prevail. They could do this.

"Yeah, let's go kill some more robots!" Herb sounded the battle cry.

The others raised their makeshift weapons. "Yeah!" they all cried.

Ichabod wasn't much for playing video games. He tolerated watching his friends play the shooter games. He never knew why they got all wound up and gung-ho. Now, as he saw the look on all their faces, he noticed they all had the same look in their eyes. He knew, he also had the same look in *his* eye.

Ichabod thought he would ask his dad for a game console when this was all over. He liked the feeling of victory.

## 22

LACTOSE INTOLERANT

Mortimer's right leg had been pulped into sausage up to his knee. He felt great!

"Cheese, stat!" Dr. Clown declared.

The nurse clown handed Dr. Clown a grater. The cheese grater wasn't clean, it was flaked with the remnants of previous gratings of cheese. Dr. Clown made no attempt to clean it off.

Nurse Clown retrieved the bowl of Mortimer's leg sausage and took it to the kitchen. Stat.

Mortimer smiled at Dr. Clown as he watched him grab Mortimer's severed hand out of a blood splattered stainless steel prep bowl sitting on the good doctor's instrument table.

The hand was coated in dark, congealed blood. It was stiffened with rigor mortis.

"Perfect," Dr. Clown said, rolling the hand around in his own hands, examining it for quality. He reached for another instrument on his prep tray and came up with a long, wooden stick, its end cut to a pointed angle. "Cut the rind, stat!"

Dr. Clown pinched the forefinger on Mortimer's old hand

between his own fingers and jammed the pointed tip of the wood stick under the fingernail.

Mortimer watched in amazement. He had lazy-minded thoughts like, this all would make a very good documentary on the cable food channel.

Dr. Clown's hands jittered as he applied pressure to the stick and pried the fingernail up from the finger. Mortimer was surprised there was so much struggle. He thought a dismembered hand would give up its nails without a fight. Dr. Clown was demonstrating that was not the case.

Dr. Clown struggled in vain. The fingernail wouldn't dislodge. The good doctor with the big red nose tried a different technique. He began to sweep the flattened end of the stick back and forth under the nail. He probed it deeper and deeper into the nail bed.

Mortimer was surprised to see goopy, congealed blood ooze out from the fingernail. Who would have thought a lopped off hand would still contain that much blood. His dizzied mind made a mental note to remember that fact in case he should ever need to use that kernel of information again. Say, if he decided to one day become an elementary school teacher he could teach that kind of thing to his first grade class during science hour. You never knew.

Dr. Clown continued to tear into the fingernail but it would not pop off. He needed a different tactic. He reached for the cheese grater. "I'll go through the rind, stat!"

Dr. Clown drew the plane of the cheese grater across the face of the fingernail. It sloughed off the surface layer of the nail, a powder of keratin appearing on the other side of the grater. Dr. Clown tapped the fingernail dust into an empty glass bowl on his prep tray. He brought the grater to his nose and took a deep sniff before working on the fingernail some more.

Mortimer's own nose got itchy looking at the tiny flakes of fingernail dust that now clung to the underside of Dr. Clown's jolly red nose. The yellow-white flakes danced around in the air currents as Dr. Clown breathed in and out.

"Fingernails are so stupid." Mortimer's inner thoughts escaped his mouth. "Like, what do they do, really? We aren't vicious animals that use them for defense or to kill prey. They are just... there! And we have to keep cutting them. Our whole lives, just cut, cut, cut. What a waste of energy and resources. Valuable resources put into growing something so useless. And we have *twenty nails*! It's insanity!"

Dr. Clown nodded as he grated Mortimer's former fingernail into cheese dust.

"I for one have had just about enough of it! Dr. Clown, I elect to have you surger my fingernails off my body. I refuse to allow these nails to rule my life any longer."

"Stat!" Dr. Clown said. And when he said it, he said it in his sexy voice.

Dr. Clown dropped Mortimer's former hand on the floor. He took Mortimer's still attached hand like a lover in the throes of passion. Dr. Clown had to have his fingernails for cheese. The attached hand was rife with living cells still nourished by the warm nail bed below.

Dr. Clown blew on the cheese grater. A cloud of dry fingernail dust bloomed in the air in front of them both. Mortimer could swear he saw the word "Love" form in the swirls of skin flakes.

Dr. Clown took the cheese grater to Mortimer's pointer finger first. He worked with a vigor reserved for artists whose muse spoke to them after a long break up. He worked the cheese grater back and forth over the nail. Mortimer watched as the nail flaked down to the nail bed in seconds.

He could tell Dr. Clown hit the nail bed because he took some nail bed with it. Mortimer was relieved to be free of the burden of the fingernail on his index finger; he had to admit having his nail bed scraped off stung like hell hosed down with vinegar. Mortimer's eyes teared but he dared not show pain for fear that Dr. Clown may not follow through with the rest of the procedure.

Dr. Clown was too engrossed in his work to notice the extreme pain his patient suffered with glee. He chiseled away the fingernail, leaving no trace of nail right to the root. He left the index finger to bleed and moved to the middle finger. He tore through that one with equal gusto.

The collection bowl was placed under Mortimer's hand. He watched the fingernail cheese pile grown like snow in a squall. He was happy Dr. Clown was making quick work of his fingernails. The pain, while intolerable, was sure to subside after a while. He could bare it. He was pretty sure he could anyway.

Before long Dr. Clown had the bowl half full of fingernail cheese (and a healthy dose of blood.) He situated his operation now at Mortimer's feet. There was sweat on Dr. Clown's brow. The operation was intense. He called out, "Sponge, stat!"

Nurse Clown hurried into the room with an oversized puff ball. Dr. Clown raised his head up from Mortimer's foot and scrunched his eyes closed. Nurse Clown walloped him in the face with the puff ball. A dust storm of talc enveloped Dr. Clown. Talc wasn't good for you but neither was the grease paint melting off Dr. Clown's face. The first rule of clowning was never reveal your true identity.

Who was Dr. Clown if he wasn't Dr. Clown. It was an existential query he dared not entertain, ever.

Nurse Clown retreated the operation room and Dr. Clown went back to work on Mortimer's toe nails.

Mortimer could only see Dr. Clown's back as he worked on releasing the cheese from his toenails. His arms were pumping away and Dr. Clown strained against muscle fatigue. He grunted like a frustrated boar in a barren truffle field.

Dr. Clown ceased the procedure. He called out, "More power, stat!"

"Stat!" Mortimer begged urgently. He feared the operation might be over if Dr. Clown couldn't get more power. How dreadful it seemed to have to carry on one more day with so much as a single toe nail. The horror!

Nurse Clown barged into the room once more. She pushed a dastardly piece of equipment in ahead of her. The machine looked like a refrigerator from the 1960's. It was drab colored. It appeared as if its panel were made of cheap linoleum tiles. There were a number of rubber hoses dangling from. Each hose ended in a nefarious looking piece of medical instrumentation. Most of them resembled a drill of one sort or another.

The instrument Dr. Clown chose from the device looked like an old steel wool pad glued to a pizza cutter.

With his weapon of choice in hand, Dr. Clown circled the body of the equipment. He found what he was looking for: the pull starter. Dr. Clown grabbed hold of the handle and gave it a firm, quick yank. The motor sputtered and fell silent. The doctor huffed and gave the cord another yank. Again the motor sputtered and almost coughed back to silence but caught a grumble that inspired it to life.

A plume of blue-gray smoke billowed from the machine as it chugged to a steady rhythm of internal combustion cycles. Dr. Clown seated himself at Mortimer's feet. He held the instrument up and depressed a lever on the side. It buzzed like an angry wasp. The scouring pad spun in a blur. The machine roared.

Mortimer saw Dr. Clown say something but the roar of his machine muffled what he was saying. No doubt he said, "stat" somewhere in there.

Dr. Clown turned his back to Mortimer and went to work on the big toenail.

Mortimer was relieved to see clouds of toenail cheese rise in the air in front of Dr. Clown. The burden of nails would soon be over.

"Thank you, doctor! Thank you!" Mortimer exalted. Then he yelped like a cat that got its tail slammed in a door. The doctor got through the nail and hit the nail bed of his big toe.

The pain was unbelievable. Mortimer's body shut down and he blacked out once more.

## 23

### SHOOTOUT AT THE ARCADE CORAL

Ichabod's platoon maneuvered back to the arcade. Mark R. was no longer near the downed helicopter.

There seemed to be less pandemonium in the lobby. The kids moved through the maze of arcade games toward the front of Reg E. Rat's. They snaked and inched their way, single file, hugging tight to the arcade cabinets.

Ichabod peeked around the corner of an air hockey table. He held back a gasp.

The crowd that was jammed up trying to escape had disappeared. In their place, a beaver dam built of bodies was piled against the front doors. To say they were bodies wasn't accurate. They were body parts. It was a wall of torsos, arms, legs, feet and noses. All of them bloodied, bruised and disfigured. All belonging to parents and children alike.

And there was Cheezy.

He stood sentry at the exit. His head scanned back and forth, sweeping 180 degrees., waiting for more victims.

They weren't the only survivors either. Ichabod couldn't see the others but he heard them. There were sobs and whimpers echoing from various corners of Reg E. Rat's. No doubt there were plenty of people who chose to hole up instead of flee. He wondered if they, too, had decided to team up and fight back.

"It's bad," Ichabod reported back.

"How bad?" Gerald asked.

"Cheezy is guarding the exit. There's a lot of dead people."

"Well, so what? We're not trying to leave. Any sign of Mark R.?"

Ichabod shook his head to indicate the negative.

He wasn't sure which was scarier, having to go through another killer robot or not knowing where Mark R. was in this place. One thing was certain, the only way out of this craziness was to find Mark R. and stop him. They'd been able to dispatch one robot but, the bully still controlled another four.

"How do we find him?" Ichabod asked the others.

Gerald shrugged and looked at Herb. Everyone looked at Herb.

"I'm not a scout, I'm the muscle," Herb told them. "We could go after the big ape. Maybe that will draw Mark R. out?"

"We don't have any ovens to cook him. I dunno if we can take one out without serious firepower," Ichabod rationalized.

"It's too bad we can't control them the way Mark R. does," Diz said, thinking out loud and not really offering a suggestion. They all turned and looked at her as if she were a genius regardless.

"That's not a half-bad idea," Gerald said.

"It's not a half-good idea, either," Albert interjected.

"How would we even control those things without having some crazy electric boxing gloves like Mark R. is wearing?" Alicia added.

"But," Ichabod reasoned, "they can be controlled, somehow, remotely. We just have to figure out how Mark R. is using those gloves to control them."

"Or," Herb said, "we could just find Mark R. and stop him."

"How do we stop Mark R. without a robot of our own?" Alicia asked.

Diz and Steve stood up from behind the air hockey table and

made their way to a row of arcade games that stood between them and Cheezy the Gorilla.

Ichabod watched, dumbfounded as they carried out some plan they hadn't discussed with anyone else. He hoped they weren't going to do something stupid. He didn't risk asking what they were up to for fear of alerting the big robot ape to their position.

Diz was on top of a Ms. Pac Man cabinet. She poked her head over the top of the console. Ichabod hoped her plan was to take a look at what the situation was for herself. Steve was on the Street Fighter 2 machine, next to Diz. He, too, spied the scene on the other side.

"What are they doing?" Alicia whispered.

"I have no idea. Just taking a look, I hope," Ichabod whispered back.

Herb looked like he was deciding if he should join the action with Diz and Steve. It looked as if they had some kind of plan and he was a boy who was drawn to action. He knew Ichabod would hunker down and wait for Mark R. to show up. That wasn't working for Herb.

Herb crawled over the arcade games on his belly.

Ichabod, Gerald, Albert and Alicia crunched closer to one another. They had no idea what to do other than watch what the others had in mind.

Before Herb could climb up on another of the arcade games, Steve jumped on top of his machine and leaped off the other side. They heard the whir of Cheezy's servo's buzz into action as soon as Steve was out of sight.

They heard Steve yelling. Then, Diz stood up on top of her machine, holding her pizza cutter aloft. She pounced off the cabinet like a lioness on the attack.

Herb rolled his eyes. They made their move without him. He scrambled up and over the video games. The battle had started without him.

Ichabod swiveled and peeked back around the corner of the air hockey table. He saw Steve facing off against Cheezy on the ground.

Diz was on Cheezy's back, her arms slung around his neck, hanging onto the pizza cutter with both hands. The business end was digging into Cheezy's neck. He couldn't see where Herb was from his vantage point.

Steve had no weapon. He was taunting Cheezy. The logic of Cheezy's programming was crossed, deciding if the bigger threat was the enemy in front or the enemy on its back. He would make a move to lunge at Steve and then his coding would dictate that the attack was from the rear. He would pull up and reach for Diz on his back but then a conflicting line of code would indicate the threat in front of him and he would lunge again at Steve.

That made hanging onto Cheezy the equivalent of riding a mechanical bull. Diz held a firm grip on the pizza slicer. The more Cheezy jerked back and forth, the more her grip would slip on the handle. She strained to grab a foothold on his back. She needed a bit more leverage and she could pull the blade into Cheezy's neck. Maybe it would sever a vital wire or something.

Steve was frozen. He knew he wanted to be brave in front of Diz. The way Diz looked at him when he whispered to her that he was gonna kick its ass made him do something funny. Or maybe stupid. But those feelings that Diz evoked, drove him to do wild things. Now he was stuck trying to kick a killer robot gorilla's ass, without a weapon.

Good thing for Steve the robot didn't know how to deal with him and Diz at the same time. That bought him time. He was able to count the beat between the robot's attention span on him and then on Diz before returning back to him. It was in those precious distracted moments he could make a move.

He just needed to figure out what that move was!

He wished the others would come help. He thought they were supposed to be a team.

But he couldn't allow that either. What if one of the others did wind up saving the day? Diz wouldn't look at him in that way that made his insides burn like a fire anymore. No way! He had to act before anyone else could steal his thunder.

And then Herb joined the fray, ready to swipe his mojo.

Cheezy reacted to the new threat. The gorilla's attention was drawn away from Steve. It was his moment. There was no way he was going to let Herb be the hero.

The robot lurched toward Herb. Then stopped and reacted to Diz tugging on his neck. His programming was fighting a battle on three different fronts now. Cheezy had a one track mind and attention deficit disorder. It was his weakness.

Steve saw the opportunity to exploit it.

A suicide mission. He counted on one more hiccup in the robot's circuits.

Cheezy reached for Diz, jolted and took another swipe at Herb.

Steve charged.

Cheezy jolted again as Steve made a run at the deadly bot. It switched gears and reached for Herb. Steve was wide open.

Steve had no plan other than to attack. The rest of the plan was formed when he spotted torn off wiring under the gorilla's foot.

Steve slid at Cheezy's feet like he was going into second base. As he slid past the robot's feet he grabbed hold of the tangle of wires. The robot adjusted and swung a fist down at him. It missed as he slid past. The momentum caused Cheezy to put his weight on the opposite foot.

The leg that Steve held went in the air and whipped Steve off the floor. Cheezy's foot slammed back down and Steve slammed down with it.

He had the wind knocked out of him and felt massive pressure on his own legs. He was pinned under the gorilla's foot and struggled to suck in air before the gorilla pounded him.

Diz held tight for the ride. Cheezy tottered from side to side. She was able to dig a knee into the robot's back and gained the leverage she sought. She reared back her weight and pulled the blade of the pizza slicer into Cheezy's neck. She heard a *pop* like electricity arcing.

Steve was pinned under Cheezy's foot. The boy's legs were broken. In the fall, his dad would rake big piles of dried, brown leaves under the old oak in their backyard. Steve would take a run at the pile and dive in. The sound of a thousand leaves crunching under his weight was satisfying. That was the exact sound the bones in his legs made when Cheezy stomped down on them. That sound was far less satisfying.

He didn't focus much on the pain in his crippled legs. The tips of the frayed wiring he still held on to sparked. They were live! Sometimes, on the weekends, his dad would throw on a late night action flick. If his mom was asleep, his dad would let him watch too, even if the movie was rated 'R'. Those action movies always had a scene with sparking wires. It meant something was shorting out. All he had to do was touch the wires to one another and, KABOOM! Just like in the movies.

Steve took half the wires in his other hand and aimed his hands at one another. The frayed ends of the bare wires touched each other and there was a loud *pop*, like a large balloon had burst, coupled with a blinding white light.

Diz yanked as hard as she could. She knew she was cutting into the killer robot. She leaned into him, intent on slicing its head clean off. She heard the loud *pop* and thought she'd succeeded. She fell backwards off the robot, realizing she'd just been zapped hard with a surge of electricity. Before she hit the ground, she saw the robot's head still intact, fire billowing out of its neck.

She hit the floor on her back. The wind was knocked out of her and she blacked out when her head bounced off the tiled floor.

Cheezy was cooked. Steve couldn't appreciate the moment of victory; he'd been electrocuted to death. Diz, too, wasn't able to savor the flavor of triumph. She was knocked out cold. But she was alive.

Ichabod, Gerald, Albert and Alicia appeared out of hiding. They marveled at the burning gorilla robot.

Gerald ran to Steve. He shook his friend's shoulders, imploring him to wake up and see what he'd done. Steve's body shook off the smoke trapped beneath his clothes. He'd been grilled from the inside out. Gerald noticed how hot his shoulders felt. He flinched away from Steve's body.

"He's gone," Gerald announced. He didn't take his eyes off Steve. He wanted to be wrong. He wanted to see Steve open his eyes and smile.

Herb cradled Diz's head in his hands. He'd watched her fall off the killer robot and saw her head bounce off the floor like a half-deflated basketball. The thought that she might be dead never crossed his mind until Gerald told everyone Steve was gone.

Herb put his ear to Diz's mouth to listen for breath. A soft breeze tickled his earlobe. The sensation gave him butterflies in his stomach. He felt guilty but he didn't care, he stole that special moment for himself before sharing with everyone else the news that she was still breathing.

"What do we do? What do we do?" Alicia asked. She panicked. She didn't know how to deal with a dead body. She'd never seen one before today. It was freaking her out. She clenched her hair in her hands and tugged. She was going to freak out!

Before she could scream, Mark R. shut her up. He stood on top of one of the birthday party tables. He raised his fist to the air and his electric glove jolted to life. Lightning orbited around it. "You fucks are dead!"

Ichabod and his friends were caught in the open. Their only cover was a burning robot.

## 24

### MARK R. IS A BIG PIECE OF SHIT

Mark R. was pissed. Those jerks weren't supposed to take out the robots. He raised his fist in the air. He felt the electricity course through his body. It tickled and made him light-headed. His hands stung and throbbed from the bulbous formation of circuit boards, wires and solder that had melted to his fists.

It hurt like hell and messed with his head but the realization that he could control the Reg E. Rat robot band with his mind made it an even trade-off.

He used his thoughts to summon Pupperoni to the lobby.

Icky Sticky and his band of smelly little shits had nowhere to run. Cheezy, the flaming gorilla, blocked the exit. Mark R. blocked the party room and the exit out the back door. He had Pupperoni coming from the arcade.

"Fuck you, Mark R.!" that jerk, Herb, called out. He was holding the girl who fell off the robot. Mark R. was pretty sure she was dead, along with the other one who stood against his robot gorilla.

"Look at you, Mr. Necrophiliac," Mark R. taunted. "You better hurry up while she's still warm. My robot fried her like a chicken nugget, that oughta give you a few extra minutes with her before she goes cold on ya."

He saw fire in Herb's eyes. He could tell the wimp wanted to take a run at him. He could also tell the little twerp was too scared to try anything. He was weakling and a coward like the rest of them.

Mark R. ruled this place. He ruled everywhere he went.

Icky Sticky and what was left of his friends huddled around near that Herb kid and his dead girlfriend. They were open targets.

Mark R. examined the lightning orbiting his fists. One of his favorite activities in school was to spit-flick kids in the hall. He'd work up a good, thick loogie of phlegm and hook his finger inside his mouth and whip it out toward some unsuspecting punk who looked at him funny. The giant goober would fly through the air and splatter the dork's face. His entire day would be ruined and Mark R. would feel better about himself for a few minutes.

Could he spit flick lightning off his gloves in the same way?

Only one way to find out.

He reared back and flung his fist side-armed at the army of dorks. A cluster of purple lighting broke free of its orbit around his fist and shot through the air, crackling until it struck the other dead kid.

The jolt of voltage struck the corpse and ignited his dead neurological synapses. The body's limbs flailed for a moment like a possessed marionette.

Mark R. cackled as he watched Icky Sticky and friends scatter for cover. He loved the look of terror he invoked. It was the exact same reaction as his spit-flicking episodes at school. Everyone scattered, they didn't want to be the next victim.

He whipped balls of lightning toward the arcade machines they'd taken cover behind. Purple bolts of electricity enveloped the cabinets they struck and sizzled the circuits inside. Smoke billowed from within the games as they cooked from the inside out. Mark R. would burn everything to the ground until Icky Sticky had nowhere to hide.

"Knock it off, Mark R. You're such a piece of shit!" one of Icky Sticky's friends called from their hiding place.

"I *am* a piece of shit!" He launched more balls of lightning at the arcade, igniting the air hockey table.

He wouldn't have to be a piece of shit if everyone just respected him. It never would've come to this if everyone had gone along with his program. He never understood why nobody liked him. After all the torment, all the beatings and bruises, he would've thought they'd all succumb to his will.

The equation was simple. If you'd be his friend, he wouldn't have to fuck with you. Why was that so difficult to understand?

They were all jerks though. Day in and day out. They never learned their lesson, just like Mark R.'s father always said he never learned his lesson.

Mark R. never understood why he should learn his lesson though. What was there to learn when his dad never even tried to teach him anything. His life at home was a torture chamber.

"You forgot to put the garbage out!" would be followed with a slap across the face. But he never asked him to take out the garbage the night before.

"There's dog shit in the living room again!" was punishable by a kick to the groin. The logic that Mark R. had been at school all day and couldn't have let the dog out didn't click because his dad was passed out drunk all afternoon.

If he didn't clean the dishes, he'd learn to wash them by getting cigarettes put out on the back of his neck. Mark R. stopped eating at home because he didn't want to create any dirty dishes. His father piled up enough in the sink as it was.

Sometimes his dad would pummel him awake in the middle of the night. He would blabber on about how it was Mark's fault he drove his mother away. Mark thought his mom disappeared because she'd had enough of the beatings.

Mark wished he knew where his mother went to go hide. He'd run away and hide with her too.

But he had nowhere to go.

He had no friends to have a weekend sleepover with and have the opportunity to escape the beatings for a day or two. Not one single buddy he could hang out with after school, long enough for his dad to pass out drunk so he could sneak into his bead without getting knocked out cold before he went to sleep.

Mark R. only knew one way to communicate his frustrations with them. He knew his father's way. He knew how to teach them all a lesson.

Mark R. flung another set of lightning balls and lit up two more arcade games. He smiled out of one side of his mouth and watched it all burn.

## 25

### THE SINGULARITY

STEVE AWOKE FROM THE DARK. He was groggy and disoriented, like he'd woken up in the middle of a dream. Something was different. He felt bigger. He felt an effortless strength he'd never possessed before. Had he been dreaming he was a bodybuilder and risen with the vestiges of that dream?

Steve sat up and heard the hum of servo motors. His eyes widened. He knew that sound. The robot! He covered his face with his arm, expecting to be pummeled by a giant robot fist.

There was no robot beast around to beat him up. There was a robot though. His own arm had fused to the remains of Cheezy. Just Cheezy's leg to be specific. The metal and wires must have melted to his skin when he shorted out the robot's circuitry.

The added weight of the leg was too heavy for Steve to bear. His shoulder gave out under the weight and his new arm dropped to the floor with a thud.

"Shit." Steve was surprised by the sound of his own voice cursing. He'd never said a bad word in his life.

A series of crackling bangs distracted him from his newfound proclivity for profanity. He hunched down behind his new leg-arm for cover. He saw several arcade games sizzle with purple lightning and billow grey clouds like a barbeque smoker.

He spied Ichabod behind the air hockey table. Ichabod was focused on something behind Steve. He glanced the other direction and saw Mark R. standing on a table in the party room. His fists glowed purple. The class bully laughed like the complete lunatic he was. Then he cast his fist toward the arcade area and a volley of purple ball lightning shot off his hand and blasted the hockey table Ichabod was hiding behind.

Ichabod crawled away from the table. He could hear a few of his other friends crying. Steve couldn't run. He was pinned down by the weight of his own leg-arm. Through the chaos he noticed something else disconcerting. Voices in his head.

They were telling him to attack. The kids were in the arcade. The voice urged him to kill. The voices were strange, robotic. He almost didn't comprehend them as voices, but impulses. Odd urges in his mind like a wizard compelling him to do something that didn't make sense.

Steve's leg-arm began to move with the compulsion of those urges. He propped himself up on his arm-leg. The motors that were somehow part of him hummed and buzzed. The leg-arm moved and dragged the rest of Steve along with it. He got on his feet and tried to keep pace with himself. It was odd but he didn't have time to comprehend what his body forced him to do.

Steve's leg-arm dragged him to the flaming arcade. He maneuvered around the maze of burning arcade games. The compulsion in his head made him seek out his friends but told him they were his enemy. He went with his leg-arm. There wasn't much choice in the matter.

He spotted Gerald running around a Ms. Pac-Man game. "Gerald! Help me!"

Gerald's head popped out around the side of the video game, "S-S-Steve?"

"It's me!" Steve cried as he was dragged toward his buddy.

He realized he must've been a sight to Gerald. Steve would've thought it would be scary to see Gerald coming at him with a giant gorilla robot leg attached to his arm. Gerald didn't freak out though. Gerald smiled at him and started to cry. He ran out from behind the game and cried Steve's name like he hadn't seen him in years.

Gerald hugged Steve. "I thought you were dead," he kept saying.

"I'm not dead," Steve said. "I'm not dead? Why would I be dead?"

"You. The robot. Mark R. You broke it. I held you. You didn't move. You were gone."

Gerald was muttering some crazy shit. Steve didn't know why and he was a little more worried about this leg being part of his body more than Gerald freaking out about some nonsense about him being dead when he was clearly alive.

"You gotta get this thing off my arm man. You gotta do it quickly before I kill you."

Gerald broke his embrace. He looked at Steve's arm. He hadn't noticed the hairy leg until that moment. Gerald was being weird. Steve was getting angry with him. He kind of did want to kill him.

"Damn. It's melted to your arm, Steve. I dunno how to help you."

"Get it off before I kill you!"

Gerald took a step back from his friend. He'd never heard him so angry. "C'mon man. Let's find the others. Maybe we can figure something out."

The dark compulsion in his mind agreed. That agreement made Steve feel better. "Yes. Take me to the others," he commanded Gerald.

*Find the kids.*
*Kick their asses.*
*Report their location.*
*Kill them.*
*Kill them.*
*Kill them.*

The compulsion ranted over and over again. Instructions, cold and clear. He could not stop the urge. He knew the only way to stop the unending commands were to carry them out to completion.

Gerald led him to Ichabod, Albert, Diz, Herb and Alicia. They were huddled under a basketball game.

*Basketball,* Steve reported.

*Kick their asses.*

*Kill them.*

*Kill them.*

*Kill them.*

The instruction list became shorter after he found his friends and thought their hiding place to the voice repeating in his head. All he had to do was kick their asses and kill them and the urges would cease.

"Steve! You're alive!" Ichabod cried out from under the basketball game.

Steve's gorilla leg-arm dragged him next to Icky. He swung his leg arm hard at Ichabod. He landed a kick-punch against Ichabod's ass.

Ichabod yelped in pain. The girls screeched. Herb said, "What the hell did you do that for?"

Steve responded by kicking Herb in his ass.

The girls screeched again and scurried out from under the game.

"What the hell did I do to you?" Herb asked Steve.

Steve answered by reaching for Herb's neck with his all human hand.

Ichabod, who'd been rubbing the pain out of his own butt cheek, saw Steve go for Herb's neck and pushed him back.

"I'm gonna kill both of you!"

Herb and Ichabod scurried like two crabs trying to get out from under the game and aways from Steve.

Steve's leg-arm stomped on Herb's leg. He was pinned down and couldn't get away.

"Why are you doing this?" Gerald asked his friend.

"I don't want to hear the voices anymore," Steve pleaded.

"What voices?"

Gerald could see the struggle on Steve's face. He was fighting something unseen, trying to compose himself.

"I can't take the voice. I have to kill," Steve growled, his face contorted and he leaned down hard on Herb's leg, trying to smash it flat.

Gerald grabbed Steve's shoulder. "Calm down man! You're scaring us."

Steve looked Gerald in the eye. The rage washed away. "I don't want to hurt anyone. Make it stop."

"It's the arm," Ichabod shouted, "he's part of the robot. The robot is still trying to kill us! It's not Steve."

Diz pushed past everyone, and wrapped herself around Steve's gorilla robot leg-arm. She produced her pizza cutter and rolled it back and forth across Steve's elbow. Steve screamed, averted his eyes and let it happen. Diz made quick work of Steve's appendage and severed it from the robot leg in seconds.

She turned and looked at the others, her face covered in blood spatter and the biggest smile on her face that Ichabod had ever seen.

## 26

### THE UPPER CRUST

Mortimer's toenails were filed down to the beds. He felt ethereal. He was becoming pizza. Who wouldn't want that?

"Crust, stat!" Dr. Clown said, handing the nurse a large stainless steel mixing bowl full of toenail cheese.

The clown nurse took the bowl of cheese on the prep tray and handed a large pizza tray over to the goofy doctor.

"Stat!" Nurse Clown said.

"Stat!" Dr. Clown said.

"Stat!" Mortimer said, delirious.

Dr. Clown focused on Mortimer's stump. It had scabbed over and become a hardened shell. Dr. Clown knocked on the scab, it sounded crunchy like the toasty crust of a fresh loaf of bread.

Dr. Clown stroked his chin, contemplating something. He raised a finger to the air and declared, "Done!"

Mortimer had faith in Dr. Clown's diagnosis. He'd become cheese and sausage and pepperoni and sauce. Now that his crust was done he'd be pizza. He couldn't wait!

Dr. Clown retrieved an instrument from his prep tray that

looked like a spackling knife. Nurse Clown looked disappointed that she wasn't asked to hand the instrument over to the doctor. Mortimer thought her face looked funny reflected in the mirror finish of the spackle knife.

Mortimer felt like saying stat. "Stat!"

Dr. Clown clapped Mortimer on the shoulder. He looked like a proud father. "Stat," he assured Mortimer and started working the edge of the spackle knife under the edge of Mortimer's leg scab.

As the scab lifted away from the wound, red hot pain surged around the stump. Mortimer bit back a scream, he didn't want to interfere with Dr. Clown's important work. If he winced, he may cause the scab to break and nobody likes a broken-crusted pizza.

"Oh yes. Stat. Stat," Dr. Clown marveled as he peeled the hardened scab away from Moritmer's wound. He sounded aroused.

Nurse Clown approached Dr. Clown from behind and pressed her cleavage in his back. She placed an arm around Dr. Clown and said, "Mmm, stat. Stat. Stat." Nurse Clown was just as aroused by the procedure.

The scab peeled halfway away from Mortimer's stump. The pace of the procedure was slowing. Mortimer thought this must have been a critical point, requiring the utmost care and attention or else the whole crust would be lost. That and the fact that he was pretty certain Dr. Clown was getting a handy from Nurse Clown as he worked. Mortimer understood, he would've been distracted as well.

The two critical care clown's exchanged soft, breathy "Stats" between one another. Dr. Clown never broke focus on the scab but he panted and gyrated as he worked the spackle knife, sloughing the scab free.

Mortimer was about to warn the doctor that he felt like he was going to break the crust when Dr. Clown choked off a single grunt, wiped the sweat from his brow and refocused on his work.

Nurse Clown stepped away from the procedure, mopping her hands with a wad of sterile gauze pads.

Mortimer felt the wound becoming wet again. He assumed fresh blood replaced the area where the scab had been removed. It hurt like hell and became itchy as well. He fought the impulse to reach down a scratch.

Dr. Clown repeated a series of 'stats' each one getting louder and more rapid as he chanted.

He cried the last one loud and proud, "Stat!" holding up the dislodged scab for Mortimer to see.

The scab was flat and round. It looked like a bleeding tortoise shell. The perfect crust.

Mortimer couldn't be happier. He was pizza now.

"Kitchen, stat!" Dr. Clown announced.

The nurse grabbed the crusty scab, slapped in on the prep tray and rolled it out of the room. Dr. Clown ran behind Mortimer and pushed the gurney he was on out of the room at full speed.

"Stat!" Mortimer yelled.

"Stat!" Dr. Clown yelled.

Mortimer watched the foot of his gurney blast the door open. It slammed into someone in the hallway. He knew because he heard the thud and a woman cry out, "Fucking ow!"

"A bad wound heals, but a bad word doesn't." Mortimer reminded the poor woman behind the door as Dr. Clown piloted his gurney down the hall in the opposite direction.

"Faster, stat," Mortimer instructed Dr. Clown. He saw the nurse ahead. Mortimer was sure Dr. Clown had it in him to beat her to the kitchen.

Dr. Clown increased speed. The bed jerked with each slap on his giant clown doctor shoes as they *slap, slap, slap, slap, slap, slap,* slapped down the hall.

They gained on the nurse. Her overstated clown ass (no doubt exaggerated by a few balloons under her short, white skirt) encouraged Dr. Clown to run faster like a carrot hung in front of a donkey.

"Oh, stat!" Dr. Clown howled like a horny wolf watching her bulbous buttocks twerk from the hard work she was putting in to stay ahead of them.

The nurse giggled looking back at them over her shoulder and rounded the corner out of sight.

Dr. Clown did not slow as he approached the turn at the end of the hall. Mortimer grabbed hard to the mattress and leaned his weight in the opposite direction. They were a human-pizza bobsled team. If this were the winter Olympics, they no doubt would have placed better than the Jamaican bobsled team.

The nurse disappeared at a right turn at the end of the hall just as Mortimer and Dr. Clown caught sight of her. Her prominent badonkadonk took a full second extra to disappear after the rest of her did.

"Stat," Mortimer encouraged Dr. Clown like a jockey.

Dr. Clown was going flat out. He counted on his patient to lean into the turn again and his patient came through with flying colors. They lost no ground on the nurse. They hit the right turn after the nurse but collided with an unseen pedestrian when they rounded the corner.

He saw the flash of a person get run down by his speeding gurney. The bed rattled over the body and Dr. Clown gave up the chase. As a doctor he was committed to his oath to never do no harm.

Mortimer thought the woman they plowed over looked just like his wife.

# 27

## OUT OF THE CLOSET

RORY BATTLED with the stupid Reg E. Rat costume. Of course the costume would give him a hard time when he was done with it. The rat's head was snagged, he couldn't remove it at all. He cursed.

He took a deep breath. Between quitting and all the ruckus coming from the party room, he must be frustrating himself and rushing it. There must have been snaps or buttons that latched. He didn't ever remember the head attaching to the body piece but maybe one of the managers had sewed them in to prevent one of those unfortunate beheadings.

The worst thing a Reg E. Rat performer could lose was his head. They called it a beheading, in corporate parlance. It was grounds for dismissal, not only for the performer but the manager on duty as well. If Reg E. Rat lost his head, it ruined all the magic.

Rory felt around his neck for snaps or buttons. He didn't feel anything obvious but he was probing through furry rat gloves. It seemed almost like the hair on both pieces had matted themselves together. Maybe he needed a knife to cut away the tangled fur.

He couldn't think of any type of knife or blade that was stored in the changing room.

The door opened behind him. When he turned to look who the intruder was he saw a knife.

The knife was followed by six kids who pushed into the changing room. One of them was missing an arm. Most of them held weapons.

Rory screamed. His worst nightmare was about to come true. He was about to get killed by a bunch of kids celebrating a birthday party.

The kids screamed. Their worst nightmare was about to come true. They'd just locked themselves in a room with another one of those killer robots.

No killing happened but, the screaming continued on both sides for a ridiculous amount of time. "Ahh!" went Rory. "Ahh!" went the kids. "Ahh!" went Rory. "Ahh!" went the kids.

Rory stopped screaming first. The kids were too scared of him to kill him. At least for right now, they may start stabbing and bludgeoning him once they figure the giant rat isn't going to kill them first. He had to break character.

"Please. Please. I'm not going to hurt you. I'm just a guy in a suit." Reg E. Rat pleaded with the kids.

The kids stopped screaming. They were surprised to hear a human voice emanate from the robot. Maybe it wasn't a killer robot.

"Reg E. Rat isn't part of the band. That's not a robot," Ichabod said from behind Steve, who used his remaining arm to menace the giant rat with his knife.

"Oh yeah, well if there's a guy in that costume then wave like this." Diz waved her arm over her head.

Rory waved his hand. The costume didn't allow him the movement to raise it over his giant rat head.

"Hop on one leg," Diz said, hopping on one leg while she continued to wave her hand in the air.

Rory hopped on one leg. He continued to wave his hand at his side.

Diz stopped, revealing her final judgement. "I'm not convinced."

"Diz, that's a guy. If it was a robot, it'd be trying to kill us already," Herb said.

Alicia stepped forward. "You wouldn't hurt us, would you Reg E.?"

Rory shook both his head and shoulders in the negative motion. That was his training kicking in, overexaggerating gestures inside the costume was less menacing looking to children. He put his gloved hands to the side of the Reg E. Rat head piece and attempted to lift it off his head again then shrugged. "I'm stuck in here."

"Have you been in here the whole time?" Gerald asked.

Rory nodded in the affirmative with his whole body. "Yes," he said, realizing that pantomiming while in the costume was ingrained in him. "What's going on out there?"

"You don't know?" Ichabod asked.

Rory started to indicate the negative with his body and stopped himself. "No. I quit. I've been hearing a lot of racket out there though."

"Racket? Racket! Yeah, there's been a lot of racket out there. I lost my fucking arm!" Steve held up his arm as if it wasn't obvious he had a bloody stump at his elbow.

"Your arm? You were dead as a doorknob, Steve," Diz reminded him.

"Doorknobs are a stupid thing to compare to death. It's not like they were alive to begin with," Herb noted.

Rory couldn't comprehend what he was seeing. The kids looked like they stepped out of a war movie. They were sweaty, disheveled and one of them looked like he took a grenade blast. "I dunno what the hell is going on out there but if you guys could help get this costume off, I'll help get you out of here and back to your moms and dads."

Gerald started crying first. "They're dead. There's no way they survived this. There's no way anyone survived this. We're the only ones left.

"Us and Mark R.," Ichabod reminded them. He began sobbing when he realized his dad, too, was dead.

"Okay. Okay, you need to calm down. Help me please. I can help you get to safety if you just help me."

"I've only got one arm," Steve yelled. Not at Rory. He was yelling at God. How could God allow this to happen to him.

Alicia hugged Steve. They cried together.

Ichabod came up to Rory. He saw defeat in the kid's eyes. It was alien to see through the mesh of the rat's head. The kid offered to help him through sobbing gasps.

Rory did the only thing he'd been trained to do with upset children. He hugged Ichabod. Usually the kids push back quickly, uncomfortable with a giant rat hugging them. This kid tried to melt into the costume. It broke Rory's heart. These kids needed more help than he did right now.

Screw the costume. He needed to get these kids out of here.

Rory pushed through the bundle of upset children. "C'mon. I'm gonna get you outta here."

Herb looked at Ichabod. "Reg E. Rat is gonna save us!"

Ichabod didn't look relieved. "I need to find my dad."

Alicia put a hand on Icky's shoulder. "Ick, he may not be," she trailed off, not knowing how to say what none of them wanted to hear.

Steve said, "My dad dropped me off. I'm sure he... I'm sure he can give us all a ride home if we need."

Rory held the door open waiting for the kids to follow him, "C'mon kids, let's get you out of here."

Ichabod and his friends trudged out of the changing room.

"What're your names kids?" Rory asked, trying to keep these kids distracted.

He listened as they called off their names one by one: Alicia, Diz (Diz? What kind of name was Diz?), Herb, Gerald, Steve (One-arm Steve, Rory nicknamed him on the spot) and Ichabod (but his friends called him Ick.) "Okay, Ick. And the rest of you too, I'm going to take you down this hallway and out the back emergency exit. Rory didn't expect to see a smoke haze in the hall when they left the changing room. There'd obviously been an explosion or something in the kitchen caught fire. It explained the chaos and why the kids were all so upset. The quickest way out would be the back door.

Rory heard a hard thumping sound up ahead. It must be the fire department hauling in their equipment. The last thing Rory expected to see through his meshed rat eyes was a giant killer robot and Reg E. Rat's one true love, Crusty Goodness.

## 28

PAGING DOCTOR CLOWN

CAMILLE ARRIVED for her appointment an hour early. Entering a doctor's office was like traveling through a multiverse. Time and space stretched out differently from regular Earth time. When the receptionist told her, "Have a seat, it'll be about a fifteen minute wait," Camille knew she was in for at least an hour.

Before she sat down she explained to the receptionist that her husband had been experiencing abdominal pains for the past few days and she'd like to make an appointment for him as soon as possible. The receptionist, who lacked the ability to smile or the emotional capacity to display empathy turned her appointment book several pages ahead and indicated the earliest possible day her husband could see the doctor would be three weeks from next Wednesday.

That wouldn't do. He was in a lot of pain. He needed to see the doctor as soon as possible. She inquired about an emergency appointment and the receptionist told her if he was experiencing pain he'd have to go to the hospital.

Camille considered arguing that her husband was a thick-headed, stubborn mule and would resist a trip to the hospital. The only way he was going to seek treatment was if he saw the doctor. When Camille looked into the cold, black eyes of the heartless receptionist, she knew there was no arguing with the dead or the dead inside. Camille, instead, thanked the receptionist (for what, she had no idea) and took a seat.

Camille thumbed through a wrinkled copy of *TIME* magazine that was several months outdated. She didn't read the articles and barely paid any mind to the advertisements. Her thoughts were with Mortimer and Ichabod. The Reg E. Rat's was just around the corner from the doctor's office. She wished she could pop in for a few moments, knowing she had all the time in the world before the doctor would be ready to see her.

But, she knew if she got up and explained to the receptionist that she was just going to step out for a few moments, the receptionist would likely remind her the doctor was sure to call for her in just a moment. He wouldn't, but it didn't matter. The receptionist would make her pay by tacking on an extra hour to her wait.

So she waited and fretted. She should have cancelled the appointment. Mortimer had been so nervous about going to the party alone. He had some sort of irrational fear about the place. Sure, it was a disgusting shit hole but, he was acting as if their lives would be in danger. She wasn't a fan of the place either. She knew she was using the excuse of the doctor's appointment to get out of having to go there anyway. She just didn't expect Mortimer would act so strongly about attending.

Ichabod was excited though. She hoped that Mortimer had settled in once he ripped off the band aid. She pulled out her cell phone and rang Mortimer. It rang until his voice mail answered. He must be doing fine if he was so busy that he didn't pick up his phone. She felt a bit better.

Camille continued to thumb through the well-worn issue of *TIME*. She became distracted by the sound of several loud thumps. It sounded like a giant knocking on a large wooden door. The seat under her rumbled with each muffled boom.

She thought there might have been construction going on in one of the other buildings connected to the doctor's office. There could've been some raucous party sounds coming from the Reg E. Rat building which anchored the strip mall the doctor's office was located within.

The door next to the receptionist's window opened and Camille's name was called out by the nurse who assisted the doctor.

Camille was impressed. The wait took under an hour. She got up and followed the nurse to the examination room. Maybe, if things were moving along at this pace, she'd be done in time to drop in and catch the last few minutes of the party.

The nurse escorted Camille into a preparatory room. There, she had her temperature and vitals taken. The nurse assured her she was in ship-shape health so far. They moved along from there through a set of double doors at the back of the office.

Camille did not expect the chaos she followed the nurse into. This part of the doctor's office was cast in shadows and dim, fluttering light. The hall was narrow. Another nurse, her face painted in clown make-up complete with a big red nose charged at them. She carried a huge stainless steel bowl and turned into a room to her right.

Behind the clown nurse came another sight. There was a doctor, also made up like a clown, high stepping in his oversized clown shoes pushing a gurney with a man that could have been the spitting image of Camille's husband had he been missing half an arm and a leg.

The duo were in hot pursuit of the clown nurse and followed her into the room off the hallway.

The clown doctor looked at Camille and the nurse. "Stat!" he said and then he was gone.

"That was my husband," said Camille.

"Oh, did he have an appointment today as well?" her nurse asked.

Camille felt disoriented. Wait, did he have an appointment? No, she was sure she was to *make* him an appointment. She just had that conversation with the receptionist, didn't she? But, that was him.

She could *swear* it was. He looked banged up and why was he missing his leg and arm and had bleeding sores?

"Do kidney stones lead to gangrene if not treated right away?" she asked.

"Huh?" The nurse was confused. "You'll have to ask the doctor."

The nurse led her further down the hall. Camille paused at the door and saw her husband and the weird clown doctor enter. There was a port hole in the door. Through it she was shocked to see a room that was out of place for this place, a kitchen. Like, a full blown, industrial sized kitchen. She saw stainless steel prep tables, deep basin sinks, refrigerators (big ones, like a queen sized mattress standing on its side,) and an industrial conveyor oven. The type used to cook pizzas. A smoldering robot dog was lying on the floor next to the oven.

"Why is there a commercial kitchen here? Are you sharing space with the restaurant?"

The nurse was annoyed and made it clear in her answer. "It's not a restaurant, it's a Birthday Fun Center."

Camille was stunned. She wanted the nurse to reassure her she wasn't seeing a working pizza kitchen. Instead, the nurse assured her not only was it a working pizza kitchen, it was the pizza kitchen for Reg E. Rat's Birthday Fun Center.

"Why is a doctor's office sharing office space with Reg E. Rat's?"

"Ma'am, if you'll just follow me, the doctor will see you in a few moments."

"Doctor?" Camille asked, her voice raised a few decibels now. "You mean like the doctor dressed up like a clown that just brought my husband into the pizza kitchen? Is he pulling double duty, treating patients and serving pizza as a birthday party clown?"

"Business is business," the nurse replied.

Camille was angry.

She disregarded the nurse. This doctor's office was a sham. She pushed her way into the kitchen. "Mort! Mort!" she called after her husband.

"Stat!" she heard someone call back. Was that Mortimer?

She followed the sound of the voice.

"Mort?"

"Stat!"

It came from around the back of the pizza conveyor oven. "Mort? Is that you back there? Are you okay?"

"Stat." The voice was weaker now.

She walked to the opposite end of the oven and found her husband still lying on the gurney, bleeding out. His skin was pale where it wasn't splattered in blood. Camille stood over him. He looked up at her, his eyes looked through her as if she wasn't there, a ghost.

"It's okay, honey. I'm here. What happened?"

"I... the birthday party... the pain... the doctor... *the cheese!*"

He was delirious. She had to get him out of here. This wasn't a medical facility. This was a madhouse.

A bell dinged on the oven. A freshly cooked pizza pie steamed on the end of the conveyor chain.

"Oh, look!" Mortimer pointed at the steaming pizza, "It's me. I'm pizza. I'm pizza!"

Camille panicked. Mortimer was going to die of blood loss if she didn't get him some real help, fast. She got behind the gurney and pushed.

"No, wait! Take me with you!" Mortimer said in an airy voice.

"I am. I am," Camille said.

Then he growled and pointed back at the pizza left sitting on the end of the conveyor, "Take. Me. With. You," he demanded.

"Honey, it's too hot. You can't eat that. We need to get you help."

Mortimer tried to sit up, "Take me with you," he said, more to the pizza than to his wife.

Camille capitulated. She found a tray and slid the pizza onto it and placed it in Mortimer's lap. If that would calm him down and stop him from resisting, then so be it. If he burned his mouth, it was the least of his worries at this point.

"Let's get out of here, Mort. Where's Ichabod?"

"Ichabod, stat!"

## 29

### MELTED CHEESE

Reg E. Rat was stopped by his one true love, Crusty Goodness. Theirs was an unnatural kind of love, shared only by the likes of Kermit and Miss Piggy. Two animals that were never meant to be but found themselves helplessly intertwined by fate and circumstance. The only problem was, Rory had no love for killer robot skunk divas.

Crusty seemed more of the scorned lover. "Kill. Kill. Kill," she said, like she was Varla in *Faster, Pussycat! Kill! Kill!* and less like her programmed Mae West "Come up and see me sometime" imitation.

"It's over!" Rory announced as Reg E. Rat.

Crusty was not pleased. She charged Reg E. Rat.

Rory felt the best offense was a good defense and ran the opposite direction. Ichabod and his friends beat feet right behind Rory. Even at a young age, they too, knew not to battle a woman scorned.

Reg E. Rat led the kids back to the party room. It was the only other means of escape. They'd gone from the frying pan straight into the fire. Blasts of purple lightning exploded around them. Mark R. used Crusty to corral them back out in the open. The closest cover they had were the long party tables. They dove for cover underneath them.

"Game over, Icky Sticky!" Mark R. said.

Crusty Goodness stomped down the hall and awaited further instruction from her programmer.

"Crusty, take out the rat. I'll deal with Icky Sticky and his shitty little friends."

Crusty stomped at Reg E. Rat, who wasn't doing a good job of hiding under the table. The girth of the costume prevented Rory from getting the hulking suit out of sight. Crusty grabbed Reg E. Rat by the leg and dragged him out. Rory was certain he was going to die as a giant rat who owned the world's worst pizzeria.

"I've only got eyes for you," Crusty said, part of her pre-programmed dialog now being used in a far more sinister manner.

Rory cursed the costume. Trapped inside, it would be his sarcophagus. Crusty tightened her grip on his ankle and he was hoisted into the air, upside down. Rory flailed. He had no idea how to fight a killer robot.

Rory hung helpless and wondered what the hell was going on? One minute he walked off the job, got frustrated by being trapped in his costume, a bunch of scared kids barged in on him, and now found himself in the middle of a war zone.

"What the hell happened to this place?" Rory asked himself, seeing the destruction upside down. "Wendy is going to get fired for sure." For some reason, that made him smile.

Two of the kids, Diz and Steve, attacked Crusty Goodness. Rory was impressed by their bravery but felt the children shouldn't be fighting killer robots. It wasn't safe. Given his predicament, he decided not to announce his reservations for now.

Steve climbed up Crusty's free arm like he was climbing his favorite tree. Crusty became distracted and didn't see Diz attack from the other side. She had a wicked blade that looked like the rocking pizza cutters they used in the kitchen. Diz arched the blade at Crusty. Rory heard a metallic *'sching'* and he was dropped on his head. The Reg E. Rat helmet cushioned his fall.

Diz cut off Crusty's hand! These kids kicked ass. Maybe it wasn't them who needed rescuing as much as Rory did. How long had hell gone into a handbasket out here on the floor while Rory attempted to quit? Now he understood why those kids looked the way they did when they ran into him in the changing room. They had the war stare. They'd seen some shit.

Rory had seen some shit now too.

Crusty whirred back and forth as if she was being bothered by a giant gnat. In a way she was, Steve was on her back now. Rory scrambled to his feet. He watched as Diz scattered back away from Crusty's swatting. She menaced the robot with her blade.

Rory needed a weapon too. He looked around. The only thing he saw was Crusty's hacked off hand. A robot hand was a good start to defending yourself against killer robots.

He pulled at the frayed ends of a tangle of wires and cables at the wrist. The fingers flexed and grasped. He squeezed the bundle and the hand made a fist.

"Reg E. Rat, my love," he heard Crusty say, more demonic in tone than when she was controlled by the computer system.

He looked up and saw Crusty swing at him. Instinct kicked in and Rory ducked under the hooking punch. He countered, punching at Crusty's face with the robot fist. The hit connected with a clang and Crusty was rocked backward.

Steve yanked hard on Crusty's neck and she was thrown off balance. She fell on her ass. Diz moved in and with another mighty slash, decapitated Crusty Goodness. Her lights flickered.

Alicia stepped in. "She's still alive! Fry her!" She torched the wires at the end of Crusty's wrist. The last vestiges of electric current that pulsed through Crusty Goodness ran into one another. Her circuits arced and popped in a blast of brilliant white light.

Alicia was thrown back. She lied stunned, tendrils of smoke rose from her hair.

"No!" Ichabod dropped to his knees at Alicia's side. "Leece! Leece!" He shook her like a can of soda pop.

Alicia stared up at the ceiling, unresponsive.

## CHAPTER 29

Ichabod was pissed.

He was going to stop this insanity or die trying. He surprised himself with his own sense of bravery. He learned that girls inspired you to do irrational things.

Mark R. was the source of all this. He was controlling the robots. He did it by melting the control equipment to his body. Ichabod needed some robotic fire power himself. He knew right where to find some.

"Ick, where're you going?" Gerald asked as the others gathered around Alicia.

Ichabod stopped. He turned and looked at his friends. "This is Christopher's birthday party. He can't open his present anymore, so I'm gonna go open it for him."

## 30

### WHY'D YOU BRING A RAY GUN TO THE PARTY

Ichabod dove under the first set of tables in the party room. Mark R. launched a set of purple lighting balls at him. They struck the tabletops, leaving black scars behind. Ick crawled on his belly like a soldier navigating an obstacle course.

He scurried with purpose. He knew where he needed to be and moved toward his target with cock-sure confidence. He heard innocuous lightning balls explode over top of him. Mark R. was being reckless. He was toying with him. If the bully really wanted to take care of him, he'd drop down off the stage and come after him under the tables. Stupid bullies never knew how to fight. All they knew was intimidation.

Ichabod intended to show Mark R. how to fight.

The presents were stored in roller bins on the far side of the party room. The Reg E. Rat birthday party hosts stacked everyone's presents inside a bin at the start of the party. When the party was over, they would wheel the bin out to the birthday kid's parent's car and load in the booty. That was one thing that was lost in the new age of factory produced birthday parties, you never got to see your friend open their presents to see if they loved or hated what you got them.

He needed to find the bin with Christopher's present inside. Ichabod knew Christopher would've loved his present but he wasn't going to able to enjoy it any longer. Ick wasn't going to let it go to waste now.

Ick's dad wasn't big on letting him play video games. He was limited to puzzle games or car racing games (as long as they were traditional racing games and nothing violent). Sometimes when he'd stop by Christopher's house, they'd play Christopher's favorite game, War Boy. Ichabod relished the precious moments when Christopher would hand over the controller and let Ick become War Boy, slashing and bashing his way through the War World. It was a first person shooter game, the type that immersed you into the world through the characters eyes.

Playing War Boy got Ichabod's blood pumping. He'd feel super guilty when he got home, knowing his dad would never approve of him playing. Ichabod would sometimes take an extra stroll around the block before going home, just to calm his amped up emotions.

That's why he wanted to get to Christopher's present. The Lazer Tazer from War Boy. He wasn't an expert at the game but he played enough to know how to use the Lazer Tazer and its capabilities.

Sure it was a toy mockup of a video game gun but Ichabod figured he had a pretty good idea how to make it come to life.

Ichabod found the bin marked for Christopher. He popped his head up and spied the presents inside. He heard Mark R. cackle. That was his tell. Ichabod ducked back down just before another lightning bolt sizzled over his head.

Ichabod popped back up and rifled through the presents. He knew which one was his by the wrapping paper. His dad let him buy the War Boy wrapping paper even though he didn't approve of the game. His dad could be super protective of him but it was little breaks of his own rules like that that made him love his dad so much. Ichabod wished his dad was here right now to keep an eye on him. Not protect him, just keep a watchful eye on him. Just in case.

Ick fished his present out of the bin before another set of lightning balls crackled overhead. He crouched back down behind the bin. He tore open the present like it was his own. Sometimes, at his own birthday parties, he already knew what the present was and would have to fake surprise. This time, even though he knew what gem lay wrapped inside, he had no need to fake the elation he felt to have War Boy's Lazer Tazer in his hands.

He dared to peek one eye over the lip of the bin. He saw Mark R. waiting for another shot, hands at his sides, charged up with purple lightning. That was the key. Mark R. melded himself to his weapon. Icky would need to do the same.

Ick took a deep breath. He gripped the Lazer Tazer as tight as he could and raised his hand up over the bin. He heard Mark R. cackle followed by the *zap* of a lightning ball being flung off his hand. A moment later, Ichabod's own hand burned with the worst pain he ever felt in his entire life.

He cradled his searing hand to his chest, a natural reflex to the pain. He fought back tears, he refused to cry. He was a warrior now. Warriors took the pain. War Boy never cried. He fought and fought until he lost one of his lives.

Ichabod forced his hand away from his body. He wanted to look at it but his body shut his eyes, sparing him from the shock of what he wanted to see. He forced one eye open despite his body fighting his eyelid back shut. Through the crippling pain he saw his hand, or what once was his hand was now a smoking mound of melted flesh fused to the pistol grip of the Lazer Tazer.

He opened both eyes wide. Seeing the transformation his hand made the pain fade into the background of all the chaos around him. Not only had his hand fused to the weapon as he'd hoped, the jolt of electricity had ignited something within the Lazer Tazer itself. Where once there were LED lights and electronic noise effect speakers were now arcs of purple electricity. They were coiled up inside the gun, pent up energy eager to be ejected and rain fury at those who faced down its muzzle.

Ichabod War Boy. He was in the game. The game was war and he was ready to wage hell on Mark R. Ick inhaled a lungful of smoky burning flesh and plastic. The ionic putrescence spurred his warrior soul. He swore he felt hair grow thick on his chest.

Ichabod jumped up from behind the bin and took aim at Mark R. A brilliant rope of purple lighting shot out of the muzzle and fired into Mark R.'s chest. The bully fell like a toppled statue.

"Woo!" Ichabod raised his Lazer Tazer fused hand to the sky. Victory was his.

Ick shot at Mark R. again. The angle was bad, Mark R. was too low to the ground to get a clean shot off and the lightning blast struck Saucy Jack's drum kit at the rear of the stage. Cymbals crashed to the floor. The percussive sound was nearly comical *bah-dum tsss*.

Saucy Jack, the alligator drummer turned killer robot, was not happy. He appeared from behind the curtain, stomping past his controller and headed straight at Ichabod.

Ichabod fled the charging robot. He shot blindly at Jack as he ran, each sloppy shot missing the mark.

Saucy Jack launched off the stage and was almost on top of Ichabod. Ichabod stumbled, and dropped to his knee. He crawled to keep his momentum moving forward, away from Saucy Jack. He scrambled to get back to his feet and get running again. Saucy Jack countered with a breathtaking spinning whip of his tail. Ichabod was swatted hard against a row or chairs.

Ichabod was dazed. He'd never been walloped so hard in his life. He tried to aim the gun in front of him, not sure where Saucy Jack was but if the killer robot came into view, he was going to fire off as many rounds as his weapon hand would allow. Ick was dizzy and his vision blurred.

Two figures appeared in front of him. They were dark silhouettes. He almost fired but recognized they were human and not giant robots. Ick was glad he didn't get too trigger happy because he heard his dad say, "Ichabod! You're okay!"

And then his mom said, "Watch out!"

And then Saucy Jack's tail whipped both his parents out of sight.

## 31

### PARTY'S OVER

Alicia was dead. Ichabod went to go play with toys. Gerald's friend, Steve, was half a cyborg. And Mark R. still had another robot at his disposal.

"Let's just go," Gerald said.

"What?" Herb said.

"Let's just go. We can't win."

"We can't just go Gerald," Diz reminded him.

"Oh, we can. Reg E. Rat said there was a back door. He killed Crusty Goodness so she's no longer blocking the hall. We can just get out of here."

"No," Herb said, "we can't just leave Ick here. It's not right. Ick is the only one willing to stand up to Mark R. Unless we stand with Ick, Mark R. is never going to leave us alone. He'll keep picking on us until we crack too."

"Or die," Diz said, crying.

"Screw that. This party is over. I'm out," Gerald said and walked away from his friends toward the hall.

Reg E. Rat blocked the way.

"Stop," the rat said.

"Move," Gerald demanded.

"I said I'd get you out of here and I'm gonna get you out of here. All of you," Rory said from within the Reg E. Rat suit.

"Then get us out of here now."

"No, your friends are right. We have to stop this first."

"We can't."

"Oh, we can. But I need your help."

"I'm not fighting no more."

"You don't have to fight anymore. Brains over brawn. I need your brains."

Rory waved the rest of the kids over to him.

Diz and Herb carried Alicia's body with them.

"I figured it out. That kid is controlling the robots."

"No shit."

"Yeah, but I know *how* he's controlling the robots. He's melded to the computer system that controlled the robot party show. We need to override the controls."

"How? Aren't the controls on Mark R.'s hands now?"

"Exactly. That's the source of his power. All we need to do is shut the power off."

"And he's powerless," Gerald said.

"And he's powerless," Rory assured them.

"Great, how do we shut off the power?" Gerald asked.

Rory shrugged. "Pull the plug?"

They all looked dumbfounded. Could it be that simple?

"Where's the control panel?" Diz asked.

"Backstage."

"Great, so we gotta get past Sparky up there?" Herb asked.

They all looked at Mark R. who, at the moment was focused on Ichabod. They could see Ichabod crouched down behind the birthday present bins across the room. Ichabod raised his hand up over the bin, holding a toy gun. Mark R. launched a lightning bolt at Ick's hand. It struck his hand, sizzling in purple energy.

A moment later, Ichabod jumped up and blasted purple lightning bolts back at Mark R. He made the gun fuse to his hand. He had lightning bolt launchers now too! Maybe the gun wasn't a toy after all.

Mark R. was down. The group wasted no time in running up on the stage. They maneuvered around the obstacle course of ruined music instruments and dashed behind the curtain backstage.

There, they came face to face with a giant alligator killer robot.

"Saucy Jack," Reg E. Rat said.

Behind them, out on the stage, they heard another blast followed by the sound of cymbals crashing. A snare drum slid on the floor into the backstage area. Saucy Jack's drum kit had just been blown up.

Instead of taking out the group, Saucy Jack pushed them aside and stomped out on stage.

Rory didn't waste any time. He ran to the controls. The kids didn't argue, they followed him to the wall where the smashed controller stood. It still crackled and popped with stray electric charges. It was very much alive despite the gaping hole in the center where Mark R. had become one with the machine.

The panel was bolted to the wall. Rory tried to use his rat hands to feel for a plug. The costume was encumbering his progress. "Hey, help me find the wire for the plug," he asked his new friends.

Diz and Herb set Alicia's body down. They all crawled and climbed around the control panel seeking out the wire for the plug.

"I don't see any plugs!" Herb called out from under the panel.

"Me neither," Diz said from the side.

"How can it not have a plug?" Gerald asked, stupefied.

"Because it's hard wired," Rory said.

"So we can't unplug it?" Diz asked on the verge of tears.

"No. Can't unplug it."

"So what do we do? Saucy Jack just went out there to help Mark R. pulverize Ichabod!" Gerald said, his voice quivering.

"We have to find the main electric panel and cut the power to the whole building." Rory said.

This concept was beyond the kids' paygrade. Rory brainstormed.

He'd worked here long enough, and should've come across some breaker panels somewhere in this place. He saw a conduit run out the top of the computer controller. He traced it up to the ceiling where it hung a ninety degree turn and ran straight out a hold over the door to the back hall.

"C'mon, this way."

Diz and Herb sighed. He picked up Alicia's corpse and followed everyone else out after Reg E. Rat, who kept moving along the hall and looking up at the ceiling. The kids had no idea what the heck he saw up there. Were there ghosts? All they saw were pipes and light fixtures.

Rory stopped in front of the door to the kitchen. It looked like the conduit line turned off that way. He traced the line with his eyes back down the hall to where it came out from the backstage area. Definitely the right line.

They ran back into the kitchen. As soon as he opened the door he was met with flames and a wall of heat. The heat was intense, just as hot on his rat suit skin as his own skin. He could see the electric panel on the wall beyond all the fire.

"It's there!" he said to the kids.

He could see they had no idea what he was talking about. They wouldn't be able to help him out on this at all. "Listen, I can see where I can cut the power. The kitchen is on fire, but I've gotta go in there. If I'm not back in a minute or two or the fire spreads out into this hall, you all need to run. Don't go back up front. Follow this hall as far as you can go. It'll change. It'll look like a different place. Like a doctor's office. That's okay. Just keep going and you will get out of here."

"But... Ichabod," Gerald said.

"Your friend is going to have to hold his own. He looks tough. He'll be okay."

They all nodded. They weren't convinced. Rory couldn't help it; he had to do what he had to do now.

The regulation Reg E. Rat costume was corporate issued. As such it had to meet certain OSHA standards and guidelines.

Namely, it needed to be fire resistant. He didn't count on the Reg E. Rat Birthday Party Fun Center corporate bigwigs to spend top dollar on fire treated material but there was a minimum requirement that he hoped like hell they'd adhered to or else they were going to have one hell of a lawsuit on their hands if he survived what he was about to do.

Rory took a deep breath. This was the last selfless act he was going to perform for this company. He was off for college after this and that was final.

Rory ran Reg E. Rat into the fire.

He didn't have experience running into fires. He expected the heat to sear his skin first. He was wrong. It was the super-heated air that filled his lungs on the first breath that gut-punched him and knocked him to his knees.

He hadn't made it but two or three steps into the kitchen.

Because he'd dropped to his knees and stopped his forward momentum, the heat getting at his skin was the second pain he had to deal with. He ran on survival instinct and kept moving.

Rory wanted to cough and choke but he knew taking another breath would be the end of him. He crawled, through tears, fighting back a coughing fit, toward the electric panel.

It wasn't more than ten feet from the door but it felt like he was crawling across the Sahara.

Sweat poured off his skin. Rory didn't think a human body could exude that much sweat. He felt like a human sponge, every drop of water in his body squeezing out. The sweat was being absorbed up by the inner liner of the Reg E. Rat costume. It felt hot and slimy against his skin.

He did his best to ignore the disgusting sensation and fought his way to the electrical panel. He'd cut the distance in half. He kept as low to the floor as the costume would allow.

Rory heard one of the kids say, "Oh my gosh, his head is on fire!" Rory would've worried about his head being engulfed in flames but the fear in the kids voice drove him forward. They shouldn't have been seeing this. He should've told them to just run away right then and there.

Rory reached out his rat-gloved hand and touched the door on the electric panel. He felt sharp heat licking at his head. Was his hair on fire? No time to worry. He pushed himself up on his knees and jumbled with the latch on the panel door. Manipulating the latch with Reg E. Rat's giant fur fingers wasn't easy. It was costing too much time. Time he didn't have.

He heard the kids crying. One of them said, "Please don't die, Reg E." through gasping sobs. Rory wanted to cry too. His hair had to be on fire, his scalp screamed in pain. He saw flames dance too close to the eye mesh on the costume. The rat head was being devoured by the fire.

He couldn't focus on working the latch. He fingers pushed hopelessly on the little metal lever. By the grace of God, the panel door popped on with a click. He'd done it, somehow.

Rory wasted no time thanking all the angels and saints for their help. He yanked the door open and started pushing as many of the circuit breaker switches to the OFF position as fast as he could.

Everything went dark. Rory didn't know if it was because he'd cut the power off in the whole building or because he'd just died.

The orange twinkle of fire all around him answered that question. He was still alive. On his back now he was looking up at the ceiling. He didn't think he was breathing any longer. His head felt like a boiling kettle. And, for some reason, he felt serene. This is what it's like to die, he thought, and smiled a smile inside the Reg E. Rat costume as big as the smile on the outside of the costume.

He was ready to die. And then his head exploded.

## 32

TIME TO GO

Ichabod wasn't happy with Saucy Jack for whipping his parents. He raised his TazerFist and blasted him. The robot was struck in the shoulder. The blast landed right at the joint and Saucy Jack lost his arm.

"Wow, Ick! That was awesome!"

Ichabod looked over and saw his mom was okay. She was slow getting to her feet but she had the biggest smile on her face. That made Ichabod feel great. His parents never let him play violent video games. To see his mother display that much pride for his marksmanship was a victory.

Camille checked on Mortimer. She couldn't say he was okay, but at least he wasn't dead. Ichabod got on his feet. He blasted the gator again. The blast struck its side and the robot jerked as its circuits sizzled. Its innards were getting fired by the surge of lighting blasts.

Mark R. responded by launching a volley of lightning balls at Ichabod. Ichabod almost forgot about Mark R. while savoring the upper hand he had on Saucy Jack. The lightning balls missed by a hair. He could feel the tingle of electricity as they swooshed past his head.

Ichabod returned fire on Mark R., who'd taken cover behind the wreckage of instruments on the stage. His blast struck the faux piano cabinet and the thin wooden veneer lit up like it was made of matchsticks.

Camille wondered how the fire inspector allowed this business to operate. The way things were bursting into flames with no fire suppression system was appalling. She was going to make a point of going down to the city hall and logging a complaint when this was all over. If she was going to get her family out of this, she was going to have to back up her boy and put an end to the bully.

"Ick! Keep shooting at the alligator. I'll take care of the kid."

Ichabod nodded. He and mom were a team now. Ick took aim at Saucy Jack and squeezed off another volley at the killer robot. He couldn't explain how he fired the Lazer Tazer fused to his hand. It was something like half thought and half clenching the jumble of flesh and melted plastic. He wasn't manipulating a mechanism, it was more like thinking, 'shoot' and the gun would go off. Just like you'd grab a ball or itch your nose without consciously thinking about it.

Saucy Jack strode at Ichabod. His programming dictated brawn over brains Ichabod assumed, or Mark R. controlling the robot thought that. Either way it was stupid.

Since he took off one arm he took aim at the other. The robot presented him with an open target. He shot again and the blaster struck true. Jack's other arm dislodged from its socket. It didn't fall off but dangled like a wet spaghetti noodle.

The robot couldn't punch but it could still stomp. Ichabod retreated to the bins of birthday presents. The robot would have to maneuver around a bunch of tables. He bought himself some extra time to set up another shot and maybe take out the alligator's legs.

Ichabod saw his mom creep on the stage toward Mark R. Mark R. was monitoring Saucy Jack's assault on Ichabod. No doubt, directing the robot's actions. Ichabod blasted a few more unaimed shots at the robot to keep Mark R.'s attention away from his mom.

Saucy Jack chose to walk over top of the tables to get to Ichabod. It wasn't a smart move. Saucy Jack's leg went straight through the table top which wasn't designed to hold the weight of one of the Reg E. Rat robot performers. They were designed to be bolted to the stage and entertain kids, not rampage the joint.

Ichabod bought more time. His mom was at the side of the stage now. Mark R. was piloting the robot out of its current dilemma. Ichabod held fire, Saucy Jack was creating all the distraction at the moment. The Lazer Tazer could get a full charge.

Mom was up on the stage, crawling on his hands and knees at Mark R. Mark R. didn't know what he had coming. Mom was going to give that bully what for! Ichabod was so happy.

Saucy Jack did something unexpected. Instead of pulling his leg up out of the hole in the table, he decided to just kick the table off his leg like it was a rubber boot. *Whoomph!* The table splintered off the alligator's leg. The shrapnel flew at Ichabod.

He tried to duck down but the move was unexpected. A big chunk of tabletop smashed his forehead. Ichabod saw stars.

He dropped down behind the bins. He didn't get knocked out but, his head was swimming. The world felt like it was going to blackout. He might've allowed his body to shut down had he not recognized the sound of a killer robot on the charge.

He held his Lazer Tazer hand in front of him ready to blast the first blur that came into sight.

He also heard the sound of a struggle. His mom and Mark R. were in a tussle.

Mom! He had to help his mother! Mark R. was so fucking mean, he would hurt his mom in a heartbeat. No way!

Ichabod got up to his feet. He wobbled, his body not yet ready to do what his gut wanted. Saucy Jack was right there. The robot brought a leg up to stomp Ichabod. Ichabod let off a blast. It struck the bottom of the robot's foot. The force of the blast spun the robot around. The stomp never landed.

Ichabod shot again, this time square in Saucy Jack's back. The robot was fully exposed from behind. He was designed as a stationary stage performer. Nobody was ever going to see his back. No plating or covering was fabricated back there. It was all exposed wires, motors, nuts and bolts. Lightning blasts entered Saucy Jack and he convulsed like he was having a seizure.

The robot went still, then fell to the ground. All the lights in Reg E. Rat's Birthday Fun Center went out at the same time. It was like someone pulled the plug on the whole operation as if to say, "Okay, kids, party's over. Time to go home."

Ichabod froze. There was an odd quiet over the place with the power out. There was an invisible hum that he didn't realize existed until the power was cut. He could only hear the crackle from the various fires which burned in the building. Since it was dark, the orange glow of the fires made the shadows dance.

"Mom!" Ichabod realized his mother was still dealing with Mark R.

He turned to see Camille kneeling over Mark R. She had the bully by the neck. She slammed Mark R.'s head against the floor like she was hammering nails into a coffin. Mark R.'s head thudded with each hard jerk. The bully was getting bullied.

Ick ran to the stage. "Mom! Mom!"

Camille kept on beating on Mark R. She was like a pit bull that snapped. She was possessed. Ichabod didn't know if he could stop her.

Ichabod climbed up on the stage. He freaked out seeing his mother in a rage.

Ichabod put a hand on his mother's shoulder. "Mom, enough!"

Camille looked over her shoulder at her son. She didn't stop pounding Mark R.'s head against the floor.

"Mom, he's had enough," Ichabod said, softer.

His mother slowed and then stopped kicking Mark R.'s ass. She didn't say anything. She sucked in a long gulp of air to catch her breath and then left Mark R. to lick his wounds.

Ichabod saw Mark R. stare wide-eyed up at the ceiling. He

wasn't sure if he was dead at first but he saw his chest rise and fall with shallow breaths. He wasn't dead, he was stunned.

Ichabod breathed a sigh of relief. As much as he wanted Mark R. to get his ass kicked, he didn't want him to die. Which was odd, Ichabod thought, because Mark R. had spent the last hour on a rampage of death. Ichabod didn't know why he took pity on him.

"It's because you're the better man," his mom said to him.

Did Ichabod ask the question aloud? No, mom's just know. She was a great mother.

They both heard Mortimer sobbing. Ichabod and Camille went to tend to him. He was upset that he was cooling off. Nobody liked cold pizza.

Mortimer caressed Camille's cheek with his remaining hand. "But what you did up there for our boy...that warmed my heart. It should've been me." The euphoria he'd felt when he became pizza had washed away. He was useless to his wife and child.

"Mort, it's okay. You're okay. We're all going to be okay," Camille assured him.

"Yeah, Dad! Mom kicked Mark R.'s ass!" Ichabod exclaimed.

"Language," Mortimer said to Ick.

"Oh, Mort, I think the boy has earned one bad word in all of this. Did you see how brave our Ick was?" She looked around at all the wreckage, dead robots and dead humans alike.

She choked back a sob. If she allowed herself to dwell on the fact that her son had faced all this carnage and had come out on top she would've lost her shit. She couldn't do that. Not now. Not after what her husband and son had seen. She'd only experienced a snippet of it, no doubt.

"Dad, we've gotta get you to a hospital."

Camille perked up. "This *is* a hospital."

"What?" Mortimer asked.

"I got here from the Same Day Outpatient Care Facility. They called me back from the waiting room and we walked down a hall and then turned and turned again and then I saw you and everything got weird. But, yeah, I was there and now I'm here. The two are connected."

"The doctors," Mortimer paused as he recollected the blur of his thoughts, "...are clowns. I remember the clowns. He removed my kidney stones and I felt great. I don't mean great, I felt *GREAT*."

"Stones?" Camille asked.

"Yeah. It was kidney stones. I went to pee. The pain was awful. Next thing I knew I was on a gurney and they said it was stones and they'd remove them. Stat."

"The clown doctors?"

"Yeah. Oh man. I felt like a new man. I never felt so good in my entire life. I was eighteen again. I was ready to do backflips. I wanted to party. I wanted to become pizza. Stat."

"You wanted to become pizza?" Camille asked.

Ichabod laughed. His dad was saying some funny stuff.

"Yeah. I was pepperoni," Ichabod raised his arm stump, "and cheese. I was the crust and sauce. I was pizza. That was great too."

"Pizza. Oh, pizza! The pizza you insisted you take along with you. That's you!"

"Ahh, ya." Mortimer said.

"Eww." Camille said. That pizza looked exactly like all the other pizza served here at Reg E. Rat's Birthday Fun Center (and Same Day Outpatient Care Facility).

"Mom, can we go?" Ichabod asked. He was tired.

"Not yet. We need to get your dad some help."

"Stat," Mortimer said.

# 33

## SEND IN THE CLOWNS

MORTIMER'S FAMILY helped him onto the gurney. Ichabod helped his mother push Dad to the hallway. It took time maneuvering the gurney around the debris scattered everywhere. The fires continued to burn. The power remained out. The robots remained lifeless.

The darkness in the smoky hall was thicker than congealed gravy. Camille used her phone for light. The hall twisted back beyond the stage door, the kitchen (where the oven and Pupperoni continued to smolder like an old camp fire), the bathrooms and then the hall turned and twisted. It got weird.

Dark gave way to light. The empty corridor became populated with doors to examination rooms.

Silence gave way to the sound of children crying.

They were the sounds of duress not associated with little kids getting injections, nor the general fear of men in white coats. The cries were of a more primal, life-fearing variety. These children were in fear of losing their lives.

Ichabod and his parents found the children huddled up in examination Room Delta. Ichabod recognized them right away: Diz,

Herb, Gerald, Steve and Alicia. Alicia was laid out on the examination table. She looked blue.

"She's dead," were the words Gerald used to greet Ichabod and his parents.

"What?" Ichabod couldn't process what he'd heard. It sounded like Gerald said she was dead.

"Oh, dear. Oh, not good. Not good at all," Ichabod's mothers fretted.

"Eh, she'll be alright," Mortimer said, waving off everyone's worry like they were overreacting.

"Mortimer, the girl is dead," Camille said, trying to nail home the severity of Alicia's condition.

"She's dead. I'm pizza. What's for lunch?"

Camille had to get Mortimer help. He'd lost his mind. PTSD was setting in already. The girl was dead, she couldn't do anything more for her. She pushed the gurney further up the hall. "Come on, Ick. We've gotta get Dad some help, fast."

Ichabod didn't want to leave his friends. Every time he did, one of them died. His dad would be okay. "No, mom. I need to stay here with them. You take care of Dad."

"There's no way I'm letting you out of my sight, Mr. Man. Let's go!"

"No mom. I can't. I've got to stay with them. I can't let *them* out of my sight." Ichabod took a step inside Examination Room Delta.

"Ick, I've gotta get your dad help. He's gone loopy. He can't handle everything he's lost."

Steve said, "Too bad you can't get him some robot limbs. Those were pretty cool."

"Huh?" Camille asked.

"Oh, sorry, Mrs. Ichabod's Mom. It's just, I had a robot arm, or foot. My arm was a robot foot. It was freaky but I felt indestructible also. I was dead but I'm alive now because of it. I guess I'm part cyborg now."

"It was weird," Gerald said.

"You're weird," Steve said.

Camille looked at Steve. She noticed a part of his arm was missing. She looked at Ichabod's laser gun hand, fused to his own hand. Man and machine. They were fusing together all over this place.

"Ichabod, I will let you stay with your friends but you've got to get me a robot arm and a robot leg. That'll get your dad fixed up."

"What about Alicia?" Steve asked.

Camille thought a moment, "Well, if you said Steve was dead and he fused a robot leg to himself to come back to life then maybe we can do the same for Alicia?"

Ichabod's eyes lit up. "Hey, yeah! That'll work. It's gotta work. C'mon, let's go guys!"

"I'm not going back in there," Diz said.

Herb nodded.

"Steve? Gerald?"

They all balked.

"C'mon. The power is out. My mom beat the shit out of Mark R. It's totally safe."

The kids all looked to Camille. They needed the assurance of an adult.

Camille smiled, proud of herself. "I kicked his ass real good. He won't be messing with you kids anymore."

Diz gasped. She took it to mean Ichabod's mom had killed Mark R. They all thought that's what she meant.

Camille saw the misunderstanding on their faces. "No. No! He's okay. It's just that he got the beating he deserved."

They kids deflated in unison. Whew!

"Okay, well, we know your dad needs a new arm and a new leg. But, what do we get for Alicia? She isn't missing anything. She's just dead," Herb said

Ichabod thought for a moment. "How'd she die, exactly?"

"I think when she got kicked in the head, I guess," Herb said.

"Well then, let's find her a head," Ichabod reasoned.

The other nodded. It made sense.

Diz brightened up. "Oh, I bet she'd love Crusty Goodness's head. That woman is all about sophistication."

Ichabod chuckled thinking about Alicia walking around with the skunk robot's head, "Yeah! Let's go get Crusty Goodness's head for Alicia!"

"And get your dad some new legs," Gerald said.

"And a new arm," Steve said. "I bet he'd look awesome with Cheezy's arm!"

They all giggled and ran off down the hall back to Reg E. Rat's Birthday Fun Center.

Camille pushed Mortimer in the exam room to prep him for surgery.

As Camille transferred a dazed Mortimer onto the examination table, a clown popped his head in the door.

"Stat?" The Clown asked for permission to help.

## 34

TURNAROUND

THE KIDS COULDN'T BELIEVE their eyes when they got back to the birthday party room. There were clowns everywhere. They were cleaning up.

A clown wearing a navy blue jumpsuit and oversized black canvas basketball shoes swept a pile of twisted metal and splintered wood into a pile in the corner. A female clown with a sad face and tear-drops painted under her eyes was clearing off whatever tables were still intact. Two bulbous, hulking clowns, wearing shorts and shirts three sizes too small for their gigantic bodies were hauling broken robot parts back onto the stage.

There were carpenter clowns rebuilding walls. There were tech clowns fixing the arcade games. There was an electrician clown that kept zapping himself over and over again, splicing two wires back together. He could've fixed the wires, but that wouldn't have been funny. Not funny at all. Zap!

All around the kids, clowns were working to get Reg E. Rat's Birthday Fun Center back in order.

A clown wearing a French Maid costume skipped by the kids.

"Excuse me," Ichabod asked, "what're you doing?"

"Cleaning up! Next party in twenty minutes!" The French Maid clown replied with flowers in her voice.

"People died here," Ichabod said.

"Nope," the French Maid clown told them. "The doctors took them away to get better. Stat!" she skipped off and went to clean something somewhere.

"Ick, this is weird."

"Yeah, weird," Ichabod said.

The bodies of the kids and their parents that had laid in ghastly heaps blocking the exit doors were gone. All the blood splatter and gore were replaced by the smell of lemon cleaner and glass doors so clean the panes looked invisible.

"We better get your dad some arms and legs before they clean them up too." Herb said, pointing to the clown maintenance staff there who were already at work piecing Reg E. Rat's Birthday Fun Center Band back together.

The kids stuck close together and walked to the stage.

"Excuse me, are there any arms or legs you aren't going to use?" Ichabod asked one of the clowns who was reattaching Crusty Goodness's swing back together.

The clown turned a wrench, then dropped it. The wrench squealed like a baby's toy when it hit the stage. "I've got arms. I've got legs. I've got torsos, fingers, toes and noses! What I ain't got, sonny, is a Skunk lady to sit on this swing here."

"So, can we get a leg and arm?" Ichabod asked. "And a Crusty Goodness's head too? It's for our friend. She's dead," he added.

The clown nodded. He reached into his coveralls and retrieved a clutch of balloons. He blew one up and twisted it a little. He blew up a second balloon and twisted in with the first balloon. He handed the balloon sculpture to Ichabod.

It was about two foot long with a knotted up ball on the end with three beans on the tip. It was a balloon animal arm.

Next he pulled out three balloons. One black, one white and one yellow. He blew up each balloon, then twisted and bent them all into one sculpture. It was a rudimentary skunk head with blond hair. He asked a clown for Crusty Goodness's head and he got a balloon sculpture of Crusty Goodness's head.

Ichabod was disappointed.

The clown blew up another set of balloons. He twisted them lickety-split and handed the second sculpture to Ick. It kind of looked like the hand except it was twisted into two sections along the long part to form a joint.

"A leg." Ichabod was less than enthusiastic as most kids were to receive a balloon sculpture from a clown.

"Crusty Goodness is over there, sir," Ichabod pointed out the spot where they'd cut her to pieces. "Thank you for the arm and leg."

The clown's face lit up. "Skunk lady!" He ran to the pile of rubble that once was Crusty Goodness. He snapped his fingers and called, "Stat!" to one of the Clown custodian pushing a broom around.

Gerald whispered, "Ick, there's robot parts all over the stage. Let's grab what we need and get out of here while that guy is distracted."

Ichabod nodded.

They slinked onstage. Diz found a leg. It might have been Pupperoni's but it lacked skin to decipher its owner. Either way it was a leg and she took it. Herb found a shoulder attached to the upper part of an arm. It was Cheezy the Gorilla's, covered in black ape hair.

"No hands?" Ichabod said, looking all around him.

"I don't see anything obvious. It's all parts of parts." Steve said.

Ichabod was so frustrated, he squeezed his arm balloon and it popped.

It drew the attention of the repair clown. "Hey! Put those back! I need them! Next party is in twenty minutes!"

The kids ran backstage with what they had.

# 35

## ICHABOD'S BIRTHDAY PARTY

Ichabod led his army down a dark corridor. Bullet's peppered their position. They crouched down and sullied forward.

Herb grunted, "I'm hit!"

Ichabod called back to Herb, "Go recharge, get back here quick!"

Ichabod was enjoying his eleventh birthday party at War Boy's Lazer Tazer arena. All his friends he'd invited had RSVP'd. His birthday party would be the talk of the entire class on Monday morning.

Best of all, Ichabod came equipped with his own Lazer Tazer. No need to borrow one from the Lazer Tazer arena folks.

Herb ran back, his Lazer Tazer photon pack, recharged. Ick led the team deeper into enemy territory.

The object of War Boy's Lazer Tazer Arena was to cross into your enemy's territory and blow up their central photon station. Ichabod had his purple team deep into the green team's zone. The arena was a three story labyrinth of twists, turns, ramps, stairs and lots of dead ends.

Ichabod and his team formed a tough offensive line and blasted the kids on the other side out of the game. If you took three hits from the enemy lasers, you were out of the arena. So far, only Herb had fallen victim once.

Ichabod crested a narrow ramp. His teammates lined up tight behind him. He crawled on his belly over the peak. He was met with a six-foot-tall killer robot.

The robot, obscured in dark shadow, backlit by neon lights from behind, buzzed as it raised its Lazer Cannon and took aim at Ichabod.

Ick gasped. He steadied his own Lazer Tazer at the killer robot and fired. His laser blasts hit true and the killer robot went limp.

"There it is! Let's go." Ick spotted the enemy photon station and charged past the robot to their goal and birthday party glory.

The killer robot whispered, "Nice job, Ick" as he ran past.

"Thanks, Dad!" Ichabod said to his cyborg father, Mortimer.

Mortimer was so proud of his son. He'd grown so sure of himself since Christopher's birthday party at Reg E. Rat's Birthday Party Fun Center. He'd seen some shit. All his friends who lived through that party did. They grew up a lot that day.

Mortimer did, too. In a different way. He was part robot now. No longer pizza. He'd been seeing a psychiatrist two times a week since the party to get past his deep depression over not being pizza any longer.

The thing that got him past it all? Camille had willed herself to take a trip over to Reg E. Rat's. Not to bring Ichabod to another birthday party over there. That would never happen again. Instead, she walked in just to buy a Rat Pie.

She brought it home to Mortimer. He ate a slice. It was cold, stale and tasteless. It was the world's worst pizza. Mortimer didn't understand how anyone could screw up pizza? From then on he got out of his funk. If that was the pizza he longed to be, he no longer wanted to be something so sad as a Reg E. Rat Pie.

When it came time to plan Ichabod's birthday party, it was a no brainer. War Boy's Lazer Tazer Arena had just opened up. Ichabod was already equipped with his own Lazer Tazer. He begged

Mortimer and Camille to keep it after the incident at Reg E. Rat's. They agreed but only after they had Doctor Clown modify it back to a harmless toy.

Doctor Clown got right on it. Stat!

A loud alarm rang out in the arena. A red light flashed three times and then the sound of a big explosion boomed out over the Lazer Tazer sound system.

"Purple Team has won!" War Boy announced to the participants in the arena.

The members on Ichabod's Purple Lazer Tazer team cried out "Huzzah! Huzzah!" raising their Lazer Tazers to the sky. It was a scene straight out of War Boy's Lazer Tazer video game.

A boy from Mortimer's Green Team walked past, his shoulders slumped, obviously disappointed.

Mortimer slapped the boy on the back, "You'll get 'em next time, Mark."

"Thanks Mr. Ichabod's Dad," Mark R. said.

Mortimer marveled at how far Mark R. had come. He no longer bullied Ichabod and the rest of his classmates. Instead, he found out being their friend and getting along was a lot easier and a lot better.

Camille had been a bit apprehensive inviting Mark R. to Ichabod's birthday but Ichabod insisted on it. He assured his mom that Mark R. was okay now. That everyone got along with him and he was actually pretty cool when he wasn't being a dick.

Mortimer warned his son about using that word but he knew Mark R. was a dick. He'd seen it first hand and there was no better word to use to describe the way he had acted.

But, Mark R. wasn't a dick anymore. He did seem pretty cool to Mortimer too. He took the Lazer Tazer defeat in stride. He knew, after eating a 100% Grade A Ground Chuck War Boy Burger and organic Sweet Potato Lazer Fries, Mark R and the rest of the Green Team would be ready for another go through the arena.

Win or Lose, they all had fun at Ichabod's birthday party.

# FRANK J. EDLER

**Frank J. Edler** is the author of many twisted novels and uncanny short stories often cited as 'laugh out loud' reads. His writing walks the fine line between horror and the bizarre. He resides in New Jersey, a land that is both horrific and bizarre. He did not attend medical or clown school but he has attended far too many children's birthday parties.

Website - https://frankedler.com
    Facebook: https://www.facebook.com/FrankJEdler
    Twitter: @Njmetal
    Instagram: njmetal
    TikTok: MrFrank732

# ABOUT THE EDITOR / PUBLISHER

Dawn Shea is an author and half of the publishing team over at D&T Publishing. She lives with her family in Mississippi. Always an avid horror lover, she has moved forward with her dreams of writing and publishing those things she loves so much.

*D&T Previously published material:*
    ABC's of Terror
    After the Kool-Aid is Gone

Follow her author page on Amazon for all publications she is featured in.
    Follow D&T Publishing at the following locations:
    Website
    Facebook: Page / Group
    Or email us here: dandtpublishing20@gmail.com

Copyright © 2022 by D&T Publishing LLC All rights reserved. No part of this book may be reproduced in any form or by any electronic or mechanical means, including information storage and retrieval systems, without written permission from the author, except for the use of brief quotations in a book review. This is a work of fiction. Names, characters, places, and incidents are a product of the author's imagination. Locales and public names are sometimes used for atmospheric purposes. Any resemblance to actual people, living or dead, or to businesses, companies, events, institutions, or locales is completely coincidental. Decay

-- 1st ed.

Reg E. Rat's Birthday Fun Center and Same Day Outpatient Care Facility by Frank J. Edler

Cover by Don Noble

Edited by Patrick C. Harrison III

Formatting by J.Z. Foster

Reg E. Rat's Birthday Fun Center and Same Day Outpatient Care Facility

Made in the USA
Middletown, DE
11 December 2022

16670566R00089